Mrs. Entwhistle Rides Again!

Doris Reidy

ISBN-13: 978-1-7291-2849-7

Dedication

To my friends of a certain age (you know who you are) who are still picking up speed.

Other books by Doris Reidy:

Five for the Money

Every Last Stitch

Mrs. Entwhistle:
When You're Over the Hill, You Pick Up Speed

Imperfect Stranger

Contents

Acknowledgments

Thanks to Robin Achille, photographer extraordinaire, for the beautiful cover photograph and to Josh Langston, designing, editing, publishing and writing genius, for stitching it all together. Thanks to my first readers who gave generously of their time and brain cells to make Mrs. Entwhistle as good as she could be. Thanks to all the people who encourage and support me on a daily basis. What would I do without you?

Floyd's Pension Bites the Dust

Mrs. Entwhistle's cheerful yellow kitchen went dark for a minute as she took in the news. She gave herself a good shake and the darkness receded. This was no time to panic.

The registered letter was written in intimidating legalese which she had to read three times, the last time out loud. It seemed to be saying that Floyd's pension would be no more. Simply put, the pension fund in which Floyd invested faithfully for forty years had gone broke. Maybe she'd got it wrong. She needed an interpreter. She'd go see Mr. Dansinger at the bank. He'd be able to explain it properly.

Mr. Dansinger looked up with a smile when Mrs. Entwhistle entered. He stood courteously, motioned her to a seat in front of his desk, asked if he could get her anything – a cup of coffee, a bottle of water? – before he sat himself and asked what brought her to the bank that morning.

"I'm trying to figure out if this letter means what I think it means," she said, handing it over.

He read the letter silently. When he looked up, his eyes were full of concern.

"I'm afraid you got it right," he said gently. "It seems Floyd's former employer didn't keep up with his share of contributions to the pension fund. Now the business is going into bankruptcy and the pension fund is broke. It's a shame. Retirees have a right to count on funds that were promised to them, and to which they contributed."

"Floyd would have a fit," Mrs. Entwhistle murmured. She could imagine his indignation – no, his wrath – if this had happened during his time on Earth. He'd planned carefully for their old age and they did without many little luxuries so their retirement years would be comfortable. Poor Floyd hadn't lived long enough to really enjoy it, but Mrs. Entwhistle was thankful for the checks that arrived faithfully month after month from Floyd's lifelong employer. Now those checks would no longer be coming.

"Will you be all right?" Mr. Dansinger asked.

Mrs. Entwhistle knew he was genuinely concerned. His father had been their banker, and when he retired, the son took over. Their families had a long history of mutual trust.

"Well, it will take some readjusting," she admitted. "That was half my monthly income."

"Of course, you have the investment accounts from the Publisher's Clearinghouse win," Mr. Dansinger said. "The funds are in your grandchildren's names, but I'm sure they and their parents would agree to withdraw money for your use."

Mrs. Entwhistle had won a million dollars from Publisher's Clearinghouse which wasn't as much money as it used to be, she'd learned. By the time she'd paid taxes and shared with friends and family, there wasn't much left. She'd had so much fun spreading cash around that she privately admitted to her best friend, Maxine, she might have gotten a little carried away.

"But how much do I need, at my age?" she'd said at the time. Now it appeared she needed more than she'd thought. But her grandchildren's accounts were off limits.

"I won't touch those accounts," she said. "I promised that money to my grandchildren to give them a good start in life, and I won't ask for it back. No, I'll have to come up with income from some other source. Let me go home and think on it."

Ordinarily, the first thing Mrs. Entwhistle did in times of trouble was call Maxine. They'd shared so many experiences over the years: school days, motherhood, widowhood, and now retirement. Mrs. Entwhistle frequently said there never was a better friend than Max. But her hand faltered as she reached for her phone. Two things she and Maxine never discussed were sex and money. They came from a generation reticent about such personal matters. The only time money had ever been mentioned between them was when Roger, Mrs. Entwhistle's aged Shih 'Tzu, was taken and held for ransom. Mrs. Entwhistle had been grateful, but she'd declined Maxine's offer of cash and handled it herself. She'd do the same thing now.

She sat down at her desk, pulled out her last bank statement and tapped numbers into the calculator. It didn't take a mathematical genius to see that Social Security income alone was not enough. Mrs. Entwhistle had never worked outside the home, but she got half of Floyd's benefit after his death. Along with his pension, she'd had sufficient funds to live on. Frugal by nature and nurture, she'd gotten along fine.

Mrs. Entwhistle believed the Bible verse that said the love of money was the root of all evil. She thought it was far better to give it away than become enslaved by it, plus there was the added benefit of having so much fun doing it. Honestly, she couldn't regret having passed along most of her winnings even in the face of this new development. Having too much seemed to make people just as miserable as having too little. The sweet spot was living comfortably without worrying about either scarcity or surplus. But half of Floyd's monthly Social Security check wasn't going to do it. She began a list of options.

Sell the house. It was a seller's market right now, but that would work against her when she went to find a new place. Was it time to consider an over-fifty-five community? Or assisted living? She did NOT need that kind of help just yet, and besides, the monthly cost was ridiculous. It ought to be called a$$i$ted living in her opinion.

She knew Maxine would offer to share her home, but both of them were used to living alone. The worst thing would be to jeopardize a precious friendship through too much togetherness, a chance she was unwilling to take. No, she couldn't live anywhere else as cheaply as she could live in this house where she'd spent her entire adult life. The mortgage had long ago been retired and taxes were low.

Sell possessions. She looked around at the worn furniture, most of it not of the antique variety. Who would want it, let alone pay cash money for it? She owned no important jewelry or sterling silver flatware. She counted the little dog fast asleep at her feet as her most valuable possession. Roger was ancient but he was such a good dog, despite a tendency to flatulence in his old age. An aroma wafted upwards towards Mrs. Entwhistle's nostrils. She waved her hand in front of her face, jerking her thoughts back to the matter at hand.

Get a job. She paused a long time over that one. At seventy-eight, soon to be seventy-nine, it seemed utterly unfeasible. She'd never had a paying job in her life, and the thought of starting now...why, what were her skills, for heaven's sake? She could clean and wash and iron, but nobody was going to hire an old lady to do that. Baby-sitting was appealing; kids fascinated her. Her dear friend, Pete Peters, had three little ones including her namesake, Cora, whom she adored. But then she remembered reality; she'd raised Diane and Tommy and wouldn't exchange that experience for anything, but oh, the work! The rising and kneeling and reaching and carrying! She knew her knees and other parts were simply not up to it.

She was stumped. It was time to call Maxine.

Maxine was at her door in no time, alerted by the stress in Mrs. Entwhistle's voice.

"Cora, what's wrong?" she demanded from the doorstep. "Don't try to deny it, something's happened. Tell me."

Mrs. Entwhistle did. Maxine's eyes grew rounder and angrier as she listened. At one point she held up her hand to signal she needed a pause and went into the bathroom. Mrs. Entwhistle heard a muffled scream, then Maxine returned serenely to her chair.

"Go on," she said.

When Mrs. Entwhistle got to the end of her short list of options, Maxine nodded. She tapped her fingertips together as she thought. "Getting a job is the best option," she said.

"But Max, I have no skills. Who'd hire me?"

"Nonsense, Cora! You are chock-full of skills. You could give cooking lessons. How many young women know how to make biscuits like yours? You could tutor children in reading, and you'd make it so much fun they'd love it. You could...why, Cora, you could write!"

"Write?"

"Remember when I had my hip replacement operation and you took over my advice column for the *Neighborhood News*? You were a hit. People loved that column."

Maxine sounded wistful. Mrs. Entwhistle knew she'd done a little too well when she filled in for her friend. She hastened to deflect that line of thought.

"They were tickled to have you back. And I couldn't have done it without following your lead, you know that."

"The *Neighborhood News* isn't the answer; it's too small to pay a reporter. But what about the *Pantograph*?"

"The daily paper? Oh, I don't think...."

"Now wait a minute, Cora, let's think it through. The *Pantograph* can't keep help, we know that. They change reporters more than some people change shirts."

"Not exactly a recommendation," Mrs. Entwhistle said.

"No, but the reason nobody stays is the pay is low and the editor, little Jimmy Jack, is a pill."

"Maxine, don't ever go into sales."

"The thing is, you could really do some good at that

newspaper. Jimmy Jack isn't the man his father was and he's floundering."

Jimmy Jack's father, James John McNamara, known to one and all as Mac, was the founding editor of the *Pantograph*. He'd started the small daily fifty years ago and built it into a thriving regional newspaper. When he'd suddenly dropped dead during his evening stroll, James John Junior, whom everyone called Jimmy Jack had taken over the family business. He was willing, but like many sons of successful men, he had no fire in his belly for the news business or anything else. Jimmy Jack was indolent, indecisive and ignorant, which Mrs. Entwhistle pointed out.

"He's pleasant, though," Maxine countered. "He could be taught. Mac meant to bring him along, he just died too soon."

"What makes you think Jimmy Jack is looking for help?" Mrs. Entwhistle asked.

"I heard just the other day that he's lost his local beat reporter. Again."

"Local beat...does that mean school board meetings and PTA bake sales? If so, just kill me now."

"You could do it with your eyes closed, Cora. It's people you know talking about the same stuff they've talked about all our lives. You'd go to a few meetings, write your articles here at home, turn them in and collect your paycheck."

"Hmmm." Mrs. Entwhistle had to admit that sounded like something she could do. She'd taught Jimmy

Jack in Sunday School when she could cow him with a look; she still had that look. It might work.

"Promise you'll at least go talk to him," Maxine begged.

"Well, I guess I could do that much," Mrs. Entwhistle said. "But do you really think...?"

"I *know* you could do it," Maxine said in a voice that signaled the discussion was over.

Mrs. Entwhistle Has a Job Interview

Jimmy Jack was happy to make time for his old Sunday School teacher. In fact, he'd have been scared not to. He told Mrs. Entwhistle to come to the newspaper office at her convenience. He'd see her whenever.

Whenever, indeed! Mrs. Entwhistle deplored such a loosey-goosey approach to a business meeting. Maybe that was something she could fix when she worked there. Jimmy Jack had always needed a certain taking in hand.

She didn't possess a resume; instead, she got out her scrapbook containing the columns she'd written for the *Neighborhood News* "Ask a Senior" column. They would have to serve as proof that she could string a sentence together well enough to report news for the *Pantograph*. For a few moments, she got lost in rereading the questions she'd received and the answers she'd given in the columns. Her mouth quirked up at the corners when she read the one about the old guy who'd liked cable television porn. Oh, that had been a good one! But this was no time for reminiscence.

Straightening her skirt, she gave herself a critical once-over in the hall mirror. It didn't feel right to be going to an important appointment without gloves or a hat, but she and Maxine had agreed it just wasn't done these days and would only frighten the young people. Still, she wore her best suit, the one she'd bought last year on sale. Her shoes were polished, she wore a touch of pink lipstick, and she smelled ever-so-faintly of lavender. She was as ready as she'd ever be. Climbing into her old Buick, she drove the six blocks to the newspaper office, parallel-parked with the skill of long experience, and presented herself at Jimmy Jack's door. His office was a glassed-in cubicle at the rear of a big open room containing several desks. She nodded to the people at the desks as she walked through; she knew them all.

"Come!" Jimmy Jack commanded when she tapped on his glass door.

He rose hastily to his feet when he saw who it was. "Please come in, Mrs. Entwhistle. It's so good to see you again. Have a seat. Can I get you anything – coffee, Co-Cola?"

"No, thank you." Mrs. Entwhistle settled herself as best she could in the strangely shaped chrome and plastic chair in front of the desk.

"Um, well, what brings you here today?"

"Why, I thought you knew. I've come about the job. The reporting job."

"For the *Pantograph*?" he asked, with an unflattering degree of surprise.

"Yes. I understand you have an opening on the local beat." Mrs. Entwhistle thought using the term made her sound like an old hand.

"Well, yeah, one of my reporters quit Friday, but I haven't advertised the position. How did you know about it?"

"Remember where we live?" Mrs. Entwhistle said, raising her eyebrows.

"Yeah, I guess word gets around. Is Tommy looking to make a change?"

"No, I'm asking for myself."

"But Mrs. Entwhistle, how old are you anyway?"

"I don't believe you're allowed to ask me that, Mr. McNamara," Mrs. Entwhistle said, fixing him with the gaze that withered him so many years ago.

"No, uh, pardon me, you're right, sorry. Please call me Jimmy Jack. It's just that you were my Sunday School teacher when I was a kid...."

"Mr. McNamara, I'll always seem old to you, and you'll always seem like a kid to me," Mrs. Entwhistle said, with one of her rare but beautiful smiles. She never smiled unless she meant it.

"It's just Jimmy Jack."

"No, indeed. If you are to be my boss, I will call you by your proper title, which is Mr. McNamara."

"Be your boss?"

"Yes. Here are some columns I wrote for the *Neighborhood News.*" She pushed the clippings across the desk.

Jimmy Jack read them. She saw him smile; then he chuckled; then he laughed aloud.

"These are good," he said, again with an unflattering degree of surprise.

"Thank you," Mrs. Entwhistle said, casting her eyes down modestly.

"You know, I guess we could give it a try. Say, a trial period of a month. That'd give you time to get your feet under you. You know everybody in town already, so it'll just be a matter of learning how to write to the paper's guidelines and work on deadline. I can't pay much." He named a figure that was indeed not much, but it was enough.

"That will be sufficient. For now," Mrs. Entwhistle said. "A month's trial period sounds about right. I'll know by then if I wish to continue."

She knew it wasn't exactly what Jimmy Jack had had in mind when he'd said trial, but it was as much a test of her preference as his. It worked both ways. They rose and shook hands. Mrs. Entwhistle filled out some forms, slipped a lanyard containing a hand-printed press pass around her neck, and received her first assignment: the school board meeting that same evening at seven.

"You can work independently," Jimmy Jack told her. "Go to the meeting, write it up at home or here, whatever you prefer, and e-mail your copy to me. You do have a computer, don't you? And you know how to send an attachment to an e-mail?"

"Yes, Mr. McNamara," Mrs. Entwhistle replied. He didn't need to know she'd just learned how yesterday.

The room was hot and stuffy, she felt it the minute she stepped inside. Her pork chop and mashed potato dinner rumbled menacingly in her stomach. Ignoring it, she walked to the front of the room where the chairman of the school board was talking to a small group of attendees. Waiting politely until their conversation was finished, she held up her badge.

"Mrs. Entwhistle for the *Pantograph*," she said.

"Mrs. Entwhistle? What are you doing here? Not that you're not welcome," Butch Smith said.

They'd known each other since Butch and Tommy, Mrs. Entwhistle's son, were four years old. Butch had come to their house to play, and she remembered that he'd had a tendency to throw sand when the children were in the sandbox. She'd washed the grit out of Tommy's hair many a time.

"Hello, Mr. Smith," she said now. "I'm the new

reporter for the *Pantograph*, and covering this meeting is my first assignment."

"You're...what, now? And for God's sake, call me Butch."

"I'm working for Mr. McNamara at the *Pantograph*," Mrs. Entwhistle repeated. "May I sit anywhere? I'd prefer a seat up front so I can hear well."

"Uh, sure, anywhere you want, Mrs. Entwhistle. When did you, I mean, did Jimmy Jack... Are you...."

"Yes," she said firmly, and took a seat in the middle of the front row. She opened her narrow notebook and set a small recorder on the floor at her feet.

"You're going to record the meeting?" Butch asked. "I don't think we've ever allowed that."

"Under the Open Records Act, I believe I can openly record a public meeting, Mr. Smith. My recorder is in plain sight," Mrs. Entwhistle said. "And really, Butch," she added confidentially, "I need the backup, at least at first. I want to be sure to get everything right." She smiled, knowing he couldn't help smiling back. She was his old playmate's mama, after all.

Butch nodded, and took his place behind the podium. He rapped the gavel three times, calling for order, and the meeting began. An assistant passed out the agenda and supplemental meeting materials. Butch began with Item One, which was a discussion of rubber mulch versus wood chips as a cushion under the playground equipment. Apparently, this was a controversial subject, and Mrs. Entwhistle's ballpoint pen flew over her notebook. After all opinions were heard in excruciating detail, the item was tabled until more information could be obtained. On to Agenda Item Two: continue using paper towels or purchase blower hand dryers for the restrooms.

Mrs. Entwhistle felt her head jerk downward as the warm room and her full stomach nudged her toward unconsciousness. She opened her eyes wide and sat up straight, determined not to disgrace herself by nodding off on her first assignment. She had a vague idea that Agenda Item Three had something to do with the Booster Club, but the details hadn't registered. Thank goodness for the recorder. She noticed that Butch's face was red and he was sweating. Well, no wonder, it must be ninety degrees in the room. He kept darting glances at her. Had she missed something?

Finally, at ten o'clock, Butch adjourned the meeting. Mrs. Entwhistle hadn't been out that late for years. She and Maxine generally confined their activities to daylight hours. She was exhausted, and only too glad to head for home and bed. Tomorrow, she'd write up her first piece as a professional reporter.

Wait; What?

Mrs. Entwhistle remembered a visit she and Maxine had once made to a carnival fortune teller, Madame Esmeralda. She'd been skeptical of Madame's crystal ball then, but she longed for it now. For as she deciphered her notes, listened to the recording and read through the supplemental material from last night's meeting, she sensed something was amiss with the school board. It had to do with the Booster Club.

She knew Butch's wife, of course, just as she knew everyone. Sissy was Simona Cicerino before she married, the daughter of Mrs. Entwhistle's secret high school heart throb, Giancarlo Cicerino. Sissy'd been president of Booster Club for years, even though she and Butch no longer even had children in the school system. Sissy ran for re-election every year and always won. Well, if you could call it winning: no one ever ran against her. Mrs. Entwhistle read the financial report from the Booster Club again. She replayed the tape of that part of the meeting several times. Something had gotten Butch agitated, but for the life of her, she couldn't put her finger on it. If she'd been wide awake... Maybe she *was* too old to be a reporter.

Nothing to do now but write up her article with what she knew for sure – a meeting so dry that puffs of dust seemed to float from her computer keys. She pressed Send and off went her first piece of local reportage, zinging through the ozone to Jimmy Jack.

"Yer nuthin' but a dang ol' snoop!"

The spittle from Booger Daniels' mouth spotted Mrs. Entwhistle's glasses. Instinctively, she wanted to back up, but she took a step forward instead. Never give ground to a bully, that's what she'd taught Diane and Tommy.

"Now Booger, calm down," she said, fixing him with her steeliest stare. It didn't work on Booger, who was about her age. In fact, he'd been a year ahead of her in school until he dropped out at sixteen.

Jimmy Jack had asked her to drive out to Booger's place and interview him about the proposed wind farm to be built on his property. Booger was past the age where he could work his forty acres, and neither of his boys showed any interest. So when an out-of-state conglomerate came sniffing around with an offer of what seemed like a fortune if he'd just let them situate wind turbines on his fallow land, he'd jumped at it.

Mrs. Entwhistle had done some Internet homework in preparation. She'd read that each turbine typically needed an acre and a half of land and generated rent of about two thousand dollars a year. She figured if Booger kept a couple of acres around his house and allowed construction on the remaining thirty-eight acres, he could fit in about two dozen turbines. That would bring him a nice little supplemental income of forty-eight thousand dollars or so a year, which he'd earn by sitting on his porch spitting tobacco juice into the Spirea bushes. She could see how it was an appealing prospect.

The prospect didn't appeal to his neighbors, however. There had been angry town hall meetings full of "dang yuppies," as Booger referred to them, saying turbines would make a constant, low frequency rumbling noise, create a maddening flicker, and cause a variety of ills including migraine headaches, seizures, panic attacks, inner ear problems, and irritability. Mrs. Entwhistle thought the group already was irritable enough. She hated to imagine what more aggravation would bring.

She'd covered a city council meeting in which Winterberry Wind Farm representatives addressed the council, speaking of waves of the future and abundant clean energy, some of which would go to the town. They promised construction jobs, and showed a video of a green, pastoral countryside in which wind turbines strode like so many giant Santas, bringing prosperity instead of toys.

Cut away all the fancy talk and what it boiled down to was, Booger wanted the money. The town wanted cheaper wind-generated energy. The neighbors wanted Booger's head on a platter. Mrs. Entwhistle just wanted a story.

"Why don't you tell me your side of it," she said, sitting on the edge of one of the porch rockers, notebook and pen at the ready.

"I don't have to tell you nothin', Cora Entwhistle. Who do you think you are, comin' around here so hoity-toity, askin' questions about my personal bidness? If you wasn't so old, I'd run your hide right off'n my propity."

"Floyd would not like to hear you talk to me like that," Mrs. Entwhistle said mildly. It did the trick. Booger looked shame-faced at the mention of his old friend.

"Well, Cora, I'm sorry, I 'pologize. I just get so dang mad when people start tellin' me what I can and can't do with my own land."

"Understandable," Mrs. Entwhistle murmured. "But you've got some neighbors who say a wind farm next door will affect them, too. How would you answer them?"

"I'd tell 'em to mind their own dang bidness," Booger shouted, his face turning red again.

"Is there any compromise that might make everyone

a little happier?"

"The only compromise I'm offerin' is take it or leave it."

"So, you're determined to go through with it?"

"Yes, ma'am." Booger crossed both arms over his bib overalls and stuck out his stubbly chin.

Mrs. Entwhistle thanked him for his time and went home to write her article.

When Mrs. Entwhistle took on the local beat, she inherited the Pantograph "Palaver." It was something she deeply regretted, but it was her assignment so she'd do the best she could with it. The Palaver was a weekly column in which citizens could sound off anonymously about whatever was on their minds. While some contributors waxed philosophical:

Those who will cheat with you will cheat on you,

and some just put out information: *My water bill was printed upside down,*

others took palavering to new heights, or depths depending on your point of view.

Every time I read one of your posts, Bama Boy, I feel my brain cells dying.

You really need to mow your yard, neighbor. You make the whole street look bad.

To the tarp thief: Hey, you stole my tarp. The sign said everything was free except for the tarp. I know who you are, mister.

Efforts to elevate this public discourse fell flat because nobody knew who was posting what, although guessing made for lively discussions at the Busy Bee Diner. Sometimes the "Palaver" column took up fully half of the editorial page on Fridays. Mrs. Entwhistle didn't know much about journalism, but she was pretty sure the "Palaver" didn't fall anywhere in that purview. She'd suggested to Jimmy Jack that it be dropped, but he said the Friday paper sold more issues than any other.

It was Mrs. Entwhistle's job to open all the e-mails, weed out the incoherent and the profane, and organize the rest. She decided to open ten a day. She could stomach ten a day, although it shook her faith in her fellow humans.

On Wednesday she read through the requisite ten, shaking her head, chuckling and generally reacting just the way the diners at the Busy Bee did, when she came to the last one. It stopped her cold.

The School Board needs to hire an auditor for the Booster Club.

The uneasy feeling she'd had after the school board meeting flooded back. Something was going on in her beat, and she was missing it. If there was anything Mrs. Entwhistle hated, it was a sloppy job, and she didn't intend to do one. She decided to talk to Jimmy Jack about it.

"Oh, I wouldn't worry about that too much," he said. He was eating his lunch at the time, and she couldn't take her eyes off the dab of mayonnaise on his upper lip. "That's just somebody whose kid didn't make the team or something. You know, parents can be fierce about their kids."

"I just think there's something amiss, I felt it at the meeting, but I can't--"

"Nah, doesn't sound like anything the paper would want to cover. Just ignore it. Forget it."

"But shouldn't I try to find out what's going on?"

"You're supposed to cover meetings and teas and things. You're not an investigative reporter. We don't even have one on the *Pantograph*; we're just a small-town paper reporting small-town news. Stick to your beat. You don't want to kick a hornet's nest, and believe me, anything to do with schools and kids can be a hornet's nest."

By now, Mrs. Entwhistle's spine was tingling. That happened when she felt she was on the brink of some kind of discovery. Jimmy Jack had again demonstrated his ignorance, indecisiveness, and indolence, but that was not going to stop her. She meant to find out what was what.

Can We Talk?

She talked it over with Maxine, of course. Max agreed that something smelled fishy. That was an expression they'd both inherited from their husbands; almost all public goings-on had smelled fishy to those gentlemen.

"How do you think I should go about investigating?" Mrs. Entwhistle asked.

Maxine thought for a moment. "I think they have to give you the financial statements and budget for the whole year if you ask. Isn't there a Sunshine Law or something that covers it?"

"Yes, I was reading up on it. The Open Records Act says citizens are entitled to public entities' reports and documents. There are exceptions; personnel matters, client/attorney consultation, stuff like that. But any citizen can request and get the financial reports. The Booster Club is a quasi-private entity, but they get some money from the school system, who get it from the taxpayers, so it would have to be included in the budget."

"What does Jimmy Jack think?"

"He thinks it's nothing, told me to just forget about it."

"But you're not going to do that, are you, Cora?"

"You know I'm not, Max."

The ladies grinned at each other. They'd been friends for a long time and knew each other well.

"I have a feeling Butch knows something, but he'd lie to protect his reputation," Mrs. Entwhistle said, "and if the Booster Club is involved, he'd lie to protect Sissy. I hate to say that about him, but I've known Butch for years. It's hard to get around someone who's willing to lie, and I'm no expert investigator. I wish I knew how to be better at it."

"You know what I'm thinking?" Maxine asked.

Together, they said, "Pete Peters!"

Not too many little old ladies had at their disposal a Deputy United States Marshall. Pete was the agent in charge of Mrs. Entwhistle when she'd been mistakenly dragooned into the Witness Protection Program. She'd saved his life when bullets flew, and a lifelong friendship had been established. She'd used some of her Publisher's Clearinghouse money to help pay the insurance deductible for his little boy's heart operation. Pete would do anything for her, and that included naming his third child after her. She reached for her phone.

"Pete, it's Cora. How are you and the family?"

"Hello! It's good to hear from you, Mrs. Entwhistle. Everyone's fine. Corrie's cutting teeth and that makes her like a little bear, but we're thankful that's the worst thing going on with the kids."

"And Ian?"

"His heart's beating like a champ. He's gained three pounds."

"Wonderful, I'm so glad to hear that. Give him a hug for me, will you? Well, Pete, the reason I called is I need your advice on how to conduct an investigation. I'm a reporter now, working for the *Pantograph*. There's something nagging at me that I need to follow up on, but I don't know how to do it. Can you help me?"

Of course, Pete could and would. They arranged a time to meet and discuss the matter.

Mrs. Entwhistle skirted Pete's understandable question: why had an almost-seventy-nine-year-old lady suddenly taken a job? When she'd laid down a chunk of her Publisher's Clearinghouse money for Ian's heart surgery, Pete had been working two jobs to try to save up for it. Mrs. Entwhistle had offered the money, insisting it was not a loan but a gift. If Pete even suspected she needed it, he'd not rest until he'd paid it back.

"Oh, I just felt I needed to be more active," she said.

"You know, get out in the community more. It's not good for old folks to be isolated."

Pete took her reason at face value. "I wouldn't have thought you were ever isolated, but you know what's best for you," he said. Nothing Mrs. Entwhistle did or said would surprise him for long. He was still slightly in awe of her.

"What I want to do is learn more about the Booster Club's finances," Mrs. Entwhistle went on. "Something isn't right; I can feel it. Should I start with interviews? And if I do, what kind of questions would I ask? If it was you, would you talk to the president of the Booster Club first, or the chairman of the school board?"

"First thing to do is get the school board's financials and study them. You're entitled to see them as a private citizen, but the response should be even faster since you represent the paper."

Mrs. Entwhistle thought it wiser not to mention that she'd been explicitly told by her editor to leave the whole thing alone.

"Go over them line by line," Pete continued. "If you see anything you don't understand, ask for the backup material. If you still don't understand it, keep digging. Follow your instincts; you've got good ones. See how much money the school system contributes to the Booster Club. Then when you've got a pretty clear idea of the school system's contribution, ask for the Booster Club's financial report."

~*~

Mrs. Entwhistle's eyes felt like they'd been dipped in acid and then rolled in grit. She took off her trifocals and pinched the bridge of her nose. It was after midnight, long past her bedtime. Roger had paced anxiously when it became apparent they weren't going to bed where they belonged; then he'd settled himself on his favorite sofa cushion with a gusty sigh and started snoring. Mrs. Entwhistle envied his unburdened little Shih' Tzu brain. Her own brain was stuffed with undigested facts that were giving her a headache.

It was the Booster Club account that was keeping her up. She wasn't an auditor, but even she could see there'd been some fancy footwork on that balance sheet. Accrual-based accounting seemed too complex a system for such a small organization. Depreciation was high – and what fixed assets were there to depreciate? The only one she could think of was the snack shack built by team fathers several years ago. Fundraising expenses were high – but how much could it cost to put on bake sales and car washes? Management and general costs were also high – supplies for the snack shack couldn't be that much, and the manager was the president of the Booster Club, Sissy Smith, and she was a volunteer. Where was the money going?

It was time to schedule some interviews.

She and Roger slept a little later than their usual early-rising time, but by nine a.m., she'd had breakfast, fed Roger, dressed, made her bed and tidied the kitchen. She took Roger for a quick walk, and then she was ready to take on the day. First, she called the insurance office where Butch Smith worked and asked for an appointment.

"Are you interested in some life insurance, Mrs. Entwhistle?" the receptionist asked.

"No, Debbie, I need to talk to Butch about something else. Has he got any time open this morning?"

"Well, I guess... Maybe I should check with him first?"

"Not necessary," Mrs. Entwhistle said firmly. "Just put me on his schedule. He'll be fine with it."

Debbie did as she was told, and Mrs. Entwhistle took a seat in the waiting area at ten a.m. sharp. Five minutes later, Butch ushered her into his office.

"Now, what's this mysterious visit about, Mrs. Entwhistle?" he asked, smiling.

"I need to ask you some questions about the Booster Club's financial statements," Mrs. Entwhistle said, unfolding the documents on his desk. She didn't miss the way his eyes flickered when he saw them. She got right down to it.

"Now here... And here... And this. Can you explain what those expenses are for? Or should I talk to Sissy?"

"No, that won't be necessary. I'll, uh, I'll look these over and...."

"I'll wait."

"It might take me a while, and I have clients coming

in ten minutes. Let me just go over these papers at home when I have time to think, okay?"

She noted that Butch's upper lip was damp although the room was chilly. There was that tingle in her spine again, but there was nothing to do but leave. As she prepared to pull out of her parking place across the street from Butch's office, she saw him hurry out the back door, get in his car and take off in spray of gravel. So much for those clients coming in ten minutes.

Booger Takes a Hit

Booger got his nickname as a tyke because of his predilection for snacks of the nasal variety.

"Ooh, Booger, stop that! He's doing it again!" his fellow first-graders would squeal.

He wasn't the brightest bubble-light on the Christmas tree, but eventually he learned to munch in private. The name stuck, however, as small-town nicknames do, even now that he was as gnarled and mossy as an ancient oak.

The thing about spending all your life in a small community, Mrs. Entwhistle reflected, is that you can never live anything down. Booger could have turned out to be another Stephen Hawking, but at home he'd still have been Booger. She knocked on his door, which could have used a couple coats of paint. The whole house could have.

After a long wait, she heard shuffling, dragging

footsteps approach. "Who's it?"

"It's Cora Entwhistle, Booger."

"Go 'way, Cora. I ain't feelin' so hot today. Don' wan' no comp'ny."

Booger's diction was always problematic, but something in the way he was slurring his words made Mrs. Entwhistle's antenna go up.

"Open the door. I won't stay long," she said.

After another long pause, the bolt slid, the knob turned and Booger stood before her in long johns so redolent she had to catch her breath. His pale face blended with white whiskers, giving him the look of a hairy full moon. Shoulders drooped as though their own weight rendered them too heavy to support, and he clutched his left arm tightly with his right hand. He looked at her mutely.

"Oh, Booger," she cried in alarm, "what's the matter?"

"Don' know. Don' feel right."

"Does anything hurt? How long have you been feeling not right?"

"Woke up like this. Arm hurts."

"Your left arm? Is it a sharp pain or an ache?"

"Feels like a cow sat on it."

"And *did* a cow sit on it?"

"Naw. Ain't got no cows no more."

"I see. We have to get you to the hospital. You need

medical care."

"No! Ain't goin' t' no hospital. Go on home, Cora."

"I can't do that, Booger. I'm calling an ambulance."

"No!" Booger reached beside the door with his good arm and produced a pump-action shotgun. "I'll shoot 'em if they come."

Mrs. Entwhistle changed tactics. "Okay, okay. Have you had your breakfast yet?"

"Ain't hungry."

"How about just a cup of coffee? That'd taste good, wouldn't it? Come out here and sit on the porch while I fix you a cup of coffee, okay?"

Booger shuffled to the nearest rocker and plopped down like a bag of wet sand. He stared into space while Mrs. Entwhistle entered his house and headed for the kitchen. She repressed an urge to scream as she navigated the narrow space between towering piles of stuff. The windows were blocked and the light bulbs either burned out or so dim that the rooms were barely lighted. She thought maybe it was just as well she was not able to see the full horror of Booger's house.

The kitchen was a nightmare. Every surface was piled with dirty dishes, the sink was backed up with gray, scummy water, and the coffee pot was, at the moment, being investigated by a mouse. Mrs. Entwhistle did scream at that, and made her way back to the porch as rapidly as possible.

"You seem to be out of coffee," she said. "Tell you

what, let's go to the Busy Bee and get a cup there. Come on, I'll drive us."

Booger seemed to have entered into a state of sleepy confusion, and didn't object to being led ever so carefully down the rickety steps and overgrown path to Mrs. Entwhistle's car. He was only wearing underwear, but it couldn't be helped. She wasn't going to rummage around in that house for his clothes. She opened the passenger side door and helped him in. Casting her eyes to heaven, she reminded the Lord that allowing Booger in her car was good for at least three LED stars in her crown. She hoped God would know how to get the stench out of the upholstery, because she'd be calling His name while she worked on it.

As soon as she got onto the highway and was able to drive at a steady pace, Booger fell asleep. His snorting, gargling snores sounded like an SOS. She drove straight to the hospital, ignoring the signs on the Emergency Department ramp that said "Ambulances Only."

"I *am* an ambulance today," she said aloud.

Her blast of the horn made Booger's head jerk up and brought nurses running. Too late, he saw where he was and let out a roar of protest. The nurses grasped him expertly and deposited him in a waiting wheelchair. Mrs. Entwhistle lowered all the car windows, gulping fresh air as she drove slowly home.

Maxine's car was in the driveway when she got to her house, and that lady herself was swaying comfortably on Mrs. Entwhistle's porch swing.

"I knew you'd show up sooner or later," she called when Mrs. Entwhistle stepped out of her car, "so I just waited. Ronnie Sue's going to give me a haircut when she gets home."

Maxine had let Roger out, and he now came to greet Mrs. Entwhistle at a fast waddle. She remembered how he used to run and then jump the last three feet into her arms. Well, they were both getting older, but to her, life was still sweet. She believed Roger thought so, too.

"So, anyway," Mrs. Entwhistle finished up her tale of adventure with Booger, "Booger's boys will have to be talked to. The hospital will let them know Booger's been admitted, but somebody needs to speak to them about long-term care for their dad. Booger will be fragile for a while – maybe from now on – and will need help. It's too bad he has no daughters. They'd know what to do. Sons can be so clueless, and if they don't have a good wife to nudge them along, they're apt to take the path of least resistance. Which, in this case, would be to believe Booger when he insists he's okay. He's definitely not, Max. That house! And he was so dirty! That all happened before he had a heart attack. It'll get even worse now."

Maxine nodded. Growing older meant facing problems like this head-on. Mrs. Entwhistle herself had had her car taken away by her children after she'd had one fender-bender too many. It had been a struggle to win back her driving privileges, and even now she was afraid to mention problems of any kind to Diane and Tommy for fear they'd start yammering about assisted living facilities again. Some day that would be necessary, and she planned to go graciously with a minimum of fuss. Then. But not now.

"So, are you going to call Nate?" Maxine asked. Nate was Booger's oldest boy and according to family protocol, should be in charge.

"I don't know about Nate," Mrs. Entwhistle said. "He was in that drying-out place last year, you know. Where's Caleb these days?"

"I believe he lives in Riverton, but I don't know his address. He's not married; maybe he'd have more time to sort out Booger."

"Hmmm. Well, I'll see if Jenny at the hospital will give me his number. She's not supposed to, but I bet she will, for me."

Ronnie Sue appeared, striding across the lawn between her house and Mrs. Entwhistle's with the energy that only youth bestows. Despite a long day in beauty school, she professed herself eager to get her hands on Maxine's beautiful white hair. In her tote bag were a cape, scissors, comb and brush, which she duly employed as she trimmed and snipped. Roger sneezed when the falling wisps of hair tickled his nose, making them all laugh. Yes, Mrs. Entwhistle thought again, life is sweet. Now if she could just figure out how to make it a little sweeter for Booger.

~*~

Caleb proved to be willing, but not particularly able. They met in the hospital family room, sitting across from each other in plush swivel chairs. Mrs. Entwhistle hoped she succeeded in keeping any hint of judgment from her voice as she described the condition in which she'd found his father.

"Dad never said anything about having chest pain," Caleb protested. "I'd have come and helped him, but he always said everything was fine whenever I called. He said he'd soon have extra money from that wind farm thing he's been talking about."

"Yes, that may well be, but it hasn't happened yet. You need to talk to your father's doctors and see what they recommend for his further care. If they send him home, you've got some work to do in that house. Did you know your dad is a hoarder?"

"A what?"

"He doesn't throw anything away, Caleb. His house is piled to the ceilings with stuff. It's a fire hazard. You'll have to clear it out and clean it up thoroughly."

There was a pause. He looked at her hopefully. "Would you...?"

"No, I'm too old. That house is a job for young people to tackle – you and your brother. You'll need a dumpster to haul away trash and then there will probably need to be repairs to the roof, plumbing and electrical systems. And when the house is fit to live in, somebody will have to take care of your dad at least for a while.

"I don't think he can afford all that."

"Yes. That's always a problem." Mrs. Entwhistle wished she still had some of that Publisher's Clearinghouse loot. Money might not buy happiness, but it sure made life easier. "It will be a hard job, Caleb, but he's your father. He raised you and Nate alone after your mom died, and that wasn't easy, either."

"Well, I'll talk to Nate. See what we can come up with."

"Make it fast. Medicare will dictate when your dad gets released from the hospital. It will decide whether he goes to rehab or home. You have to be ready, because when those payments stop, the hospital will boot him out double-quick, and then he's going to be your responsibility."

Just the Facts, Ma'am

You never knew what went on behind closed doors, Mrs. Entwhistle and Maxine agreed. For instance, long-married couples who seemed so devoted and serene – why, they could be tearing each other's hair out in private.

"Any time I think a person has never had troubles or problems in their life, it turns out they've been dealing with a catastrophe," Mrs. Entwhistle said.

"It's true," Maxine responded. "So it's always a good idea to be gentle with people, isn't it?"

"You're better at that than I am," Mrs. Entwhistle said. "I try to be more like you, but I guess it isn't in my nature."

"Oh, now," Maxine protested, but she looked pleased.

"So, when I talk to Sissy Smith, be gentle?"

"I think so. It looks like her life is perfect: long, happy marriage, raised two nice kids, comfortable life, community volunteer. But we don't really know how she feels."

"I know something's not right," Mrs. Entwhistle said. "I hope to find out more tomorrow when I meet with her."

"Does Jimmy Jack know you're interviewing her?"

"Nope. And if he finds out and asks me about it, I'll just say I'm catching up with the daughter of an old classmate. Which is true. Partly, anyway."

The friends were silent for a moment, recalling their encounters over the years with Giancarlo Cicerino. Football hero, sports car driver, dater of prom queens, Giancarlo had cut a memorably wide swath through high school, at least among the girls. Floyd never liked him; he called him Sissy-Pants Cicerino. It wasn't really like Floyd to be unkind, and he'd never said why – just that he had his reasons.

In later years, Giancarlo had moved to California and embarked on a series of marriages that made it necessary for him to continue to earn money well into his twilight years. Some of the means he employed to get that money were less than savory. She wondered if his daughter was walking in his footsteps.

There were too many inexplicable discrepancies in the Booster Club's reports, and Mrs. Entwhistle knew that each and every one was like a ticking bomb. Why did it matter so much? Because it was a small-town institution, supported by the hard-earned money of generations of fervent football fans. Because it was an issue of trust. Because theft was a crime. The whole town turned out for the Friday night games, even organizing caravans for out-of-town matches. Football was huge and people took it seriously. A large amount of cash poured into the Booster Club through dues and fund-raising. But Mrs. Entwhistle couldn't figure out what happened to it, and people had a right to know if it was being mishandled. Where was it? That's what she meant to find out.

~*~

Sissy looked like her mother. Giancarlo's first wife, whom he married right out of high school, was a beauty. Homecoming queen, prom queen, Miss Firecracker, Miss Cotillion, she had it all, plus Giancarlo for a while. The marriage lasted long enough to produce Sissy, who was now in her fifties with grown children, and still looked terrific.

Mrs. Entwhistle hated to admit to herself that she felt a little intimidated by the woman who sat across from her in the booth at the Busy Bee Diner. Sissy was, as always, perfectly dressed, coiffed and accessorized. Her make-up was flawless, her lipstick matched her nail polish, which coordinated with her necklace. Mrs. Entwhistle thought people who looked like Sissy must never pull a weed or paint a room, let alone clean up cat vomit or toilet-train a toddler.

The waitress poured coffee and Sissy ordered a

scone, which was even more maddening. Apparently, she could afford to eat high-calorie sweets between meals and still keep her figure. Mrs. Entwhistle motioned the waitress back and ordered a scone herself. What the heck.

"I work for the *Pantograph* now," she began, "and I'm covering the School Board and all school activities."

That wasn't entirely true; there was a two-man team of sports reporters who covered the games and meets. But it was true enough for today's purpose, which was to get Sissy talking.

"I know you've been president of the Booster Club for years now," Mrs. Entwhistle continued, "and that has to be a lot of work. I wanted to ask you what you think your biggest accomplishment has been. So far."

Sissy looked at her blankly. Her stack of silver bracelets rattled as she set down her cup. "Well," she said, "I guess attendance at the games and things."

"Oh, yes, people really turn out for the home team, don't they? Does the Booster Club still get a percentage of ticket sales?"

"Just a very small percentage," Sissy said. "Mostly the club is funded by dues and fund-raisers."

"I see. And did the Booster Club build the new ticket kiosk?"

"No, that was the Junior Achievement Club. They have a Christmas raffle every year to raise money for the school."

"How nice. Good to see youngsters supporting their school, isn't it? How about the remodel of the locker room? Booster Club pay for that?"

"No, that was in the school budget...."

Sissy's voice trailed off and her eyes narrowed. Uh, oh, Mrs. Entwhistle thought, she just woke up and smelled the coffee.

"Why are you asking me all these questions about funds?" Sissy said.

"I've been looking over the Booster's Club's financials, and for the life of me, I can't figure out where the money goes," Mrs. Entwhistle said, trying for a helpless, tinkly laugh. "Of course, I'm not good with figures. I was hoping you could help me."

But Sissy was having none of it. She gathered her purse, plunked her huge sunglasses on her nose and suddenly remembered she had another appointment. Her hasty exit created such a breeze that Mrs. Entwhistle could smell her perfume for a couple of minutes after she left. The waitress arrived just then with the scones.

"Guess Sissy had to go," the waitress said, looking at her departing back. "Shall I take her scone away?"

"No, just leave it," Mrs. Entwhistle said. What the heck.

Halfway through the second scone, she was abruptly joined by Butch. He slid into the seat opposite her and wasted no time.

"What the hell, Mrs. Entwhistle? Why are you

grilling my wife about the Booster Club's finances?"

"Hello, Mr. Smith."

"And cut that out! I've always been Butch; what's with the Mr. Smith crapola?"

"When I represent the *Pantograph*, I use proper titles."

"Well, you might want to check with Jimmy Jack on that. I just talked to him, and he doesn't know what you're up to, either. Look, you leave Sissy alone," Butch said, his voice rising. "She's done a lot for this community, and she doesn't need your shit. You seem to think you're some kind of hot shot journalist now, but you're just an old lady with a big nose. Keep it out of my business."

With that withering warning, Butch extricated himself from the booth and strode out of the Busy Bee. Inquisitive glances followed him, and those at nearby tables who'd overheard what he said looked at Mrs. Entwhistle to see how she was taking it. If they expected tears, they were disappointed. She wore a tiny smile of satisfaction. The pot was being stirred exactly as she wanted. But maybe she *had* better go talk to Jimmy Jack.

"Mrs. Entwhistle, I thought I told you to let the school thing go," Jimmy Jack said, fiddling with his stapler and not meeting her eye.

"You sure did, Mr. McNamara," Mrs. Entwhistle said cheerfully. "But you know, I just couldn't do it.

Something's going on. Don't you want to know what it is?"

"Uh, well..." Jimmy Jack looked miserable. Mrs. Entwhistle knew it was just his ignorance, indolence, and indecision talking. He really didn't want to take on a controversy.

"Mr. McNamara," she said, fixing him with the old Sunday School eye, "you are running a newspaper. Your mission, as stated on the paper's masthead, is 'Truth and Justice for All.' If we expose malfeasance in one of the town's institutions, we are serving truth and justice. And if we don't – well, the truth always comes out sooner or later. How would it look for your father's newspaper to be asleep at the switch and fail to do its duty? People donate money to the Booster Club; they support its fund-raisers; a percentage of their ticket money goes to it. Don't those people deserve to have their hard-earned and freely-given money accounted for and used for its intended purpose? Isn't keeping track of local institutions what the *Pantograph* is all about? What would your father do in this situation?"

Jimmy Jack had, by now, slid so far down in his chair he was almost under his desk. He seemed ready to weep. "But Butch and Sissy," he began, "how can we accuse them?"

"It is our job to report the facts, not to make judgments," Mrs. Entwhistle said. She consciously tempered the sternness in her voice. No point in destroying Jimmy Jack. "If the facts lead to their total exoneration, why, so much the better. I'd love to be wrong."

Jimmy Jack made an effort to sit up straight and square his shoulders. "You're right; my dad would follow up on this. Carry on, Mrs. Entwhistle. But, uh, please try not to make waves."

It wasn't exactly a ringing endorsement, but she said, "Thank you, Mr. McNamara. You are a man of courage."

Mrs. Entwhistle believed in the efficacy of praise. She'd found it to be a great heartener, although in this case she suspected the effect would be only temporary.

An Old Flame Returns

Mrs. Entwhistle watched Giancarlo Cicerino step off the little prop puddle-jumper plane and carefully descend the steel steps to the runway. His suitcase awaited him on the ground, and he picked it up with a grimace. She bet he'd forgotten there were no Skycaps at his hometown airstrip. Settling her press pass lanyard around her neck, she walked forward to meet him as he entered the Quonset hut that served as the terminal.

"Well, if it isn't Cora Entwhistle!" Giancarlo said, panting slightly. "I didn't expect a welcoming committee."

"That's good because I'm not one. I'm here in an official capacity."

"Why would a pretty girl like you want to get all official on me?" Giancarlo smiled the heartbreaking smile that used to work wonders. Mrs. Entwhistle considered herself immune to it ever since their high school class's fiftieth reunion at which he'd tried to sell reverse mortgages to anyone who'd talk to him.

"I work for the *Pantograph*," she said, holding up her press badge.

"At your age?" Giancarlo was so surprised he lost his customary oily tact.

"Yes, at my age. We all need to meet our needs as best we can," Mrs. Entwhistle said. "As I assume you are meeting your needs now by making this trip home. What brings you here?"

"Why, just a little trip to see my daughter," Giancarlo said. "Nothing unusual about a father and daughter reunion, is there?"

"It's just that you come home so seldom," Mrs. Entwhistle began.

A shrill cry cut off any further conversation. Sissy launched herself at her father, nearly knocking him off his feet with her hug.

"Oh, Daddy, I'm so glad you've come! Wait, what's *she* doing here?" Sissy cast a baleful eye at Mrs. Entwhistle.

"Just leaving," Mrs. Entwhistle said, waving cheerfully. "I'll catch up with you later, Giancarlo."

She felt two pairs of eyes burn holes in her back as she left.

~*~

Mrs. Entwhistle's next stop was the hospital to visit Booger. She found him looking cleaner and pinker than she'd seen him in ages, propped up in bed watching television. She handed him the chocolate milkshake that was her standard hospital visitation gift and settled into a chair by his bed, resigning herself to listening to him slurp. At last, he came up for air.

"Mmm, thanks, Cora. Hospital food could kill a fella. They got me on this special diet, no salt and no fat and no taste."

"How are you feeling?"

"Not bad. Purty good, really. I ain't felt good in so long, I kinda fergot what it's like."

"Well, getting enough blood pumped to your brain has got to help. I'm glad you're better; you gave me a scare. Say, Booger, I wanted to ask you some more about the wind farm. Can you talk about it without getting all riled up?"

"Funny 'bout that. I take these little red pills now, and I don't get upset like I used to. Sure, fire away."

"Who are the investors who made you the offer to put the turbines up?"

"Winterberry Creek Wind Farms is what's on the papers they give me, named after the creek on my land, I guess."

"Funny they'd name their business after your creek. I thought they were from out of town."

"So'd I."

"Hmmm. Do you think there are local investors in it, too?"

"Dunno. Don't care, as long as I get my money. Need it more than ever now that I'm sick. Caleb's out at the house spendin' it like he had it. Puttin' on a dern new roof by hisself, and haulin' stuff away without even askin' do I still want it."

Good for Caleb, Mrs. Entwhistle thought.

"I'm goin' home tomorrow, and Caleb, he said he's stayin' with me for a while. Gonna take me to heart ther'py. He's outta work right now, so he can do it. And Nate's comin' Saturday."

"You're lucky to have such good boys. What do they think about turning the land over to wind farming?"

"They don't care one way or 'nother. I hoped one of 'em would wanna farm it, but nope."

Booger sounded remarkably philosophical about his dashed hopes. Mrs. Entwhistle gave a round of silent applause to those little red pills. She said, "Would it be all right with you if I'd go see Caleb at the house and look at the paperwork you were given by the Winterberry Creek folks? I'm working on an article for the *Pantograph*."

"You ain't gonna stir it all up agin, are you?"

"It's still stirred, I'm afraid. People might settle down if they knew more about the deal. I always think the more people know for sure, the less they imagine."

"Go on, then. I'll tell Caleb to let you look."

~*~

Mrs. Entwhistle followed the sound of the nail gun to the back of the house, where Caleb was finishing up the new roof. He was bright red and wet with sweat when he climbed down the ladder to shake her hand.

"Must be two hundred degrees up there," he said, taking the bandanna from around his forehead and wiping his face with it. "But look at the new roof – I did every bit of it myself. It was leaking pretty bad. I don't know why Dad never said anything about it."

"You're a good son, Caleb. I'm proud of you, and your Dad is most appreciative."

Caleb laughed. "I don't know how much he'll appreciate the inside. Come see."

The house was almost completely cleared. The exposed walls and floors were filthy, but Caleb assured her that he and Nate would tackle the dirt on Saturday. Booger would be established on the front porch so he wouldn't inhale dust while they washed and painted walls and replaced the smelly old carpet with clean sheets of vinyl. Caleb had already dealt with the kitchen, and while it wasn't up to Mrs. Entwhistle's standards, it was at least sanitary and mouse-free as far as she could tell. Still, to be on the safe side, she declined Caleb's offer of iced tea.

He had unearthed the Winterberry Creek Wind Farm's information package and handed it over to Mrs. Entwhistle, saying his dad had given the okay.

She sat in a wooden rocker and read through the literature. No wonder Booger was so determined to go through with this deal! It sounded like God was creating the wind farm on the eighth day. Peace, prosperity and free power were all promised. The artist's renderings of the big windmills set among glowing green acres were downright painterly. This was no standard brochure; it had been created for Booger's farm.

Mrs. Entwhistle paid special attention to the tiny print. There had to be an address for the company somewhere. Ah, there it was, and it was local, just as she'd suspected. She copied it down in her reporter's notebook, thanked Caleb again, and drove to the location, a nondescript office building off the interstate. Parked across the street, Mrs. Entwhistle waited. Her patience was rewarded after an hour when Giancarlo and Sissy came out, heads together, talking heatedly.

A Brick Short of a Load

Crash!

Roger sprang to his feet and barked. Deaf as he was, he'd heard *that*. Mrs. Entwhistle jumped out of bed and descended the stairs, not forgetting to hold onto the hand rail despite how hard her heart was pounding. No need for a broken hip at this stage of her life. In the middle of her kitchen floor lay a brick. She closed the door to keep Roger out so he wouldn't cut his paws, then stepped carefully around the shards of glass from the broken window, A closer look revealed a note held around the brick by a rubber band. She removed it and read, "Next one will be aimed at your head if you don't quit snooping."

Mrs. Entwhistle peeked around the curtains, but not a creature was stirring on the street. Whoever had thrown that brick must have been on foot; otherwise, she'd have heard the car take off. She didn't believe the intent was to get inside the house. Her security system consisted of an old lock that could be popped open with a credit card, if she even remembered to lock it in the first place. And Roger, of course. Roger used to be a good watch dog, but age had taken its toll on his hearing. She heard him snuffling at the kitchen door and went to get the broom and dustpan to clean up the glass so she could let him in. Then she boiled water for tea. There would be no more sleep this night.

Obviously, her inquiries were rattling someone. Mrs. Entwhistle reviewed the likely suspects: Butch, Sissy and Giancarlo. She couldn't imagine the suave Giancarlo stooping to such a brutal act, and Sissy wouldn't want to risk breaking a fingernail. That left Butch. It grieved her to think the little boy who'd played at her house could have such ill feelings for her now. But desperate people did desperate things. She decided not to take it personally. Butch had just moved up from throwing sand to throwing bricks.

Tomorrow she'd get the guys at the hardware store to put in a new window pane. She'd tell them she accidentally broke it herself; she didn't want Tommy or Diane to hear about this. So far, they didn't even know she was working for the *Pantograph,* and the longer they remained ignorant, the better. She could just imagine the worried meetings if they knew she was no longer getting Dad's pension. They'd fuss about her being too old to have a job, especially as a reporter. Then they'd offer to chip in, and that was the last thing she wanted. She and Maxine had talked it over and agreed that the best thing you can do for your children is not need their help. Diane and Tommy had been happy to accept the money she'd given them from her Publisher's Clearing House winnings, and she'd been happy to give it. That's what mothers are for. She knew they'd help her in the same spirit, but it would be a hardship at their stage of life, and she hoped it would never be necessary.

Daybreak found her sipping her third cup of tea on the porch swing, watching the sun top her neighbor's magnolia tree. The beautiful white blossoms were as big as dinner plates, but Mrs. Entwhistle knew the ground beneath the tree was nature's trash bin of yellowed leaves and twigs. Magnolias looked pretty, but you didn't really want one in your yard.

That got her to thinking of Sissy and Butch. Could it be their marriage was like that magnolia – looking good if you didn't look too closely? It was her job to stir around in all the junk under that pretty tree. They wouldn't like it, and ordinarily she'd have walked a mile out of her way to avoid getting involved in other peoples' messes. But she was a reporter now. Truth and Justice for All. Mrs. Entwhistle didn't waste much time on regrets, but she allowed herself to hate – just for a minute – that she might be the one to kick over a beehive and release a swarm of bees that would sting the whole town.

~*~

After some thought, Mrs. Entwhistle decided not to

mention the brick incident, as she called it in her mind, to Jimmy Jack, either. He was barely on board with her investigation; this might push him completely out of his comfort zone. Characteristically, she decided to go directly to the source. Placing the brick and note in a plastic grocery bag, she drove to Butch's office, presented herself to his receptionist and announced she needed a minute of his time.

Debbie looked up with evasive eyes. "Sorry, he's not available at the moment."

"Is he in?"

She couldn't lie to Mrs. Entwhistle's face. "Well, I mean, he's busy, he's not to be disturbed."

"Okay, thanks," Mrs. Entwhistle said, and marched to the closed office door, opened it and confronted Butch at his desk.

"Hey, I said no visitors," Butch said.

"And here I am anyway," Mrs. Entwhistle said. "I need to talk to you about this brick." She set the brick and note in the middle of Butch's blotter.

"I don't know anything about that," Butch said, but he couldn't look her in the face.

"Butch. I know you tossed this brick through my window last night. I'm coming to you instead of the police because I know you're not a bad person. I don't want to get you in trouble, but I won't allow you to act like this. Now tell me what's going on. What would drive you to do such a thing?"

Butch's eyes suddenly filled with tears. The sight of the normally composed middle-aged man weeping tugged at Mrs. Entwhistle's heartstrings, but she took a firm hold of herself. Actions had consequences, after all, and they were frequently unpleasant.

She said. "It isn't like you. You're obviously pushed to the limit right now. I know you wouldn't have done it if you were in your right mind."

"It's Sissy," Butch said, gulping and knuckling his eyes. For a second, he looked so like the little boy in the sandbox that Mrs. Entwhistle could almost feel the grit sifting into her hair.

"What's Sissy done?"

"We haven't been...getting along, I guess you'd say. Seems like nothing I do is right anymore. She's on the phone with her dad every time I look around, and that's not good for her. Well, you know Giancarlo. He's a slippery dude, getting worse as he gets older. They're cooking something up, but she won't tell me a word about it." Butch paused and shook his head. His expression hardened. "Look, I'm not saying another word. You'll use whatever I say for your articles. Just leave me alone. Leave this whole thing alone, or you could get hurt."

"Now, Butch. Don't get carried away. I'm not going to stop digging, so you might as well save your threats. I've known you far too long to be afraid of you. If you don't want to talk to me, talk to someone you trust to give you good advice. Get a lawyer if you need one. Just don't try to scare me off again, or I *will* go to the police. That kind of news about the chairman of the school board would travel fast."

Mrs. Entwhistle was tired. She wasn't one to while away the days on the sofa, but she was accustomed to pacing herself. Old people work thirty minutes and rest an hour, she always said. It was different now that her time was no longer her own, and she had a schedule to keep. She was spending far more time than she'd bargained for on *Pantograph* work.

"But, to be fair, that's my own fault," she said to Maxine.

They had just returned from the Garden Club tea, which Maxine attended as a member and Mrs. Entwhistle as a reporter. Mrs. Entwhistle had duly noted the names of all the ladies in attendance, kept track of who baked what, and jotted down the name and topic of the speaker ("The Garden as a Metaphor for Life," by Hazel Voight.) She was ready to write her article for tomorrow's paper, but at the moment, all she wanted was a little nap. She and Maxine wore light-weight, summery dresses and white sandals, but they were still a bit wilted from the heat.

"Go ahead and put your toes up, Cora," Maxine said. "I'll take Roger out for a wee and then I'll run along home. You take a nap, hear?"

Mrs. Entwhistle gratefully complied, stretching out under the ceiling fan in her bedroom. When she awoke, the sun had lost some of its fierceness, and there was a refreshing breeze. She and Roger walked around out in the yard, Mrs. Entwhistle inspecting her garden and Roger checking for traces of the evil chipmunk that taunted him daily.

She came to a gap in the even smile of bricks lining a flower bed. "Ha! He used my own brick to throw through my window!" she said to Roger. Roger made a great show of sniffing the area, but she knew he was only going through the motions. His senses of smell, hearing and taste were greatly diminished, but he was a polite little dog, and if she was interested, he was interested.

There was a footprint in the damp garden soil. Mrs. Entwhistle thought what a great clue it was and considered for a minute trying to make a cast of it. But then she remembered that she needed no clues to know who the brick-throwing culprit was, and anyway, how did one go about making a cast of a footprint? It sounded like a messy business.

Which led her back to contemplating what was causing Butch to act like a maniac. Something to do with Sissy and their marriage, he'd told her that much. Mrs. Entwhistle had found over her long life that there were three main suspects when a marriage went sour: sex, children and money. The Smith children were both independent adults, living successful lives; no black sheep to worry about there. As for sex, if either Butch or Sissy were having an affair, the town gossip mill would grind out all the juicy details before the sheets cooled. No, it was almost certainly money. Butch's insurance agency seemed to be doing well. As far as she knew, neither he nor Sissy had a gambling problem or a shopping addiction.

Mrs. Entwhistle's spine tingled again. It was all connected to the Booster Club, and whatever it was, it was bad enough to cause a middle-aged school board chairman to lob a brick through an old lady's kitchen window.

"Palaver" Points to Ponder

It hardly seemed any time at all since she'd read the last ten submissions to the *Pantograph* "Palaver," but here it was, time to do it again. The wind farm controversy had stoked the fires of self-expression; people e-mailed anonymous comments by the dozens. Mrs. Entwhistle knew that, theoretically, a technical person could find the identity of the e-mailers, but it was the last thing she wanted to do, even if she'd been able. It was bad enough to know her fellow citizens were capable of writing such drivel, and it would be even worse to know who they were. She had to live in this town, after all.

She scanned through the comments.

"I love a good wind farm next door, said no one ever."

"Put your darn dog up at night, or I'll bark under your window at five a.m. when I have to get up."

"To the person who took the pot of red geraniums off

my front steps – I know who you are."

And then, *"'Treasures of wickedness profit nothing: but righteousness delivereth from death.' Proverbs 10:2 You've been warned."*

It wasn't unusual to receive Scripture verses in the "Palaver" e-mails. This was the Bible Belt, after all. But something about this verse made Mrs. Entwhistle shiver a little. Maybe she'd not print that one. It seemed almost like a threat.

The next e-mail, obviously sent on the heels of the Bible verse, brought her up short: *"If you keep stealing from this town, there will be vengeance."*

That was definitely a threat, and in plain language, too. She imagined the thief reading it and knowing it was aimed at him. Or her. The sender was using the "Palaver" column to convey a message, to stir the pot. Mrs. Entwhistle hesitated, thinking hard. Maybe stirring the pot was exactly what was needed. She included both messages in the column.

Friday morning, the Busy Bee was, as its name indicated, abuzz. Newspapers open to the "Palaver" page were spread on most of the tables, and excited conversations bounced off the walls. The waitresses could hardly keep up with the requests for coffee refills and more donuts. Gossip apparently whetted all kinds of appetites.

Mrs. Entwhistle sat with Jimmy Jack in the corner booth at the back. She'd insisted he leave his office and see for himself the furor the column was creating.

"Maybe you shouldn't have run those two items," Jimmy Jack said, looking around uncomfortably at his neighbors. "We don't want to cause trouble."

"Mr. McNamara, that's exactly what a newspaper does want to do when there's a suggestion of wrong-doing. How would your father have handled it?"

"Dad? Oh, he'd have jumped in with both feet," Jimmy Jack said. A nostalgic smile spread across his face. "Dad loved a fight, always did. But I'm not like that." The smile was replaced by a look of apprehension. "But I wish you'd stop throwing my father in my face. I'm the editor now, and I don't want to cause a big stink. We don't even know there's been a theft, let alone what or where."

"Remember the **Pentagon Papers**?" Mrs. Entwhistle said. "It took moral courage to pursue that line of inquiry."

"Well, we're hardly Woodward and Bernstein," said Jimmy Jack with a rueful laugh. "I distinctly remember telling you to concentrate on teas and meetings."

"And I've covered every one of 'em," Mrs. Entwhistle said. "This is extra, this story. I just know there *is* a story here, and I feel certain it involves the Booster Club and the school board."

"Butch and Sissy again. You have a real grudge against them."

"I have no such thing. I've known Butch and Sissy all their lives, and their parents, too. But the people who give their money are owed the truth. It's time for an audit, and I mean a serious audit done by an outside accountant."

"Butch would be the one to call for that, and he never will," Jimmy Jack said.

"He will if there's enough pressure brought to bear," Mrs. Entwhistle said, fixing Jimmy Jack with a meaningful stare.

Predictably, he wilted. "What am I supposed to do about it?" he whined.

"You write an editorial calling for an audit. And if one editorial doesn't get the ball rolling, you write a second. And a third. You keep the heat on until something is done."

"Butch will never speak to me again. And what if you're wrong?"

"I hope I am. But somebody is trying to bring this matter to the attention of the community. People can deal with the truth, even if it's unsavory. Lies are what tear us apart."

They were interrupted then by people peppering Jimmy Jack with questions, eager to learn if he had any inside information he hadn't shared about the "Palaver" comments. Mrs. Entwhistle took advantage of the stir to slip away. Jimmy Jack needed to be seen standing on his own feet. But she had little hopes that he'd write those editorials. Indolent, ignorant, and indecisive, she reminded herself. *You knew that when you took this job.*

~*~

Giancarlo was waiting for her on her front porch when she got home. Somehow, she wasn't that surprised to see him. Finding people waiting on her porch had lost its novelty. She said hello, then let Roger out for a pee before she settled down on the porch swing beside her old classmate.

"What brings you to see me today?" she asked.

"I think you know, Cora," Giancarlo replied.

"No, I'm afraid you'll have to tell me. Not selling reverse mortgages again, are you?"

"Cut it out," he said shortly. "I'm here to tell you to lay off Sissy. Leave her alone. You understand me?"

"My goodness, I don't think I've inflicted myself on Sissy very much at all. Just asked her a few questions for an article I'm working on for the paper."

"Yeah, that's what I mean. You got her all upset. I don't like for my daughter to be upset."

"True, none of us like for our children to be upset. It happens sometimes, though, doesn't it?"

"I'm not going to tell you again. You know what you have to do. Quit playing reporter and remember who you are – just a nosy old lady who's about to get herself into a whole lot of trouble."

Giancarlo stalked to his car, or rather, Sissy's car, for he'd flown in from California and didn't have wheels of his own. His threatening demeanor was marred by the fact that he was a slight, small man. Mrs. Entwhistle was surprised to notice how thin Giancarlo had become. She'd not thought about it before this minute.

He spun out of her driveway too fast, braking hard to avoid getting hit by the Fed Ex truck. It wasn't like him to be so *gangsterish,* she thought. He'd always traded on his charm, and it'd served him well. His out of character behavior indicated how upset he was.

Mrs. Entwhistle thought if one more person told her she was a nosy old lady, she might start to believe it.

Mrs. Entwhistle was surprised to hear Caleb's voice when she answered her phone.

"Can you come see Dad?" he asked. "He's asking for you, seems kinda upset. He wanted to get in the car and come to your house, but he ain't supposed to drive yet."

"Of course, I'll come," Mrs. Entwhistle said. "When's a good time?"

"Well, now, actually. I can't get him to settle down 'til he talks to you."

Mrs. Entwhistle sighed. She'd been looking forward to working in her garden this afternoon. The weeds were crowding out the zinnias, and zinnias were her favorite flowers. Reporting was a tougher job than she'd imagined. But she always finished what she started, and besides, Booger was a friend. She drove to the farm, where she found him pacing on the porch.

"You wanted to talk to me?" she said, holding onto

the porch column as she climbed the steps. Maybe she should start carrying her cane again.

"I gotta tell you somethin'. I ain't gonna rest until I get it off'n my chest."

"Well, here I am. Tell me."

"Those wind farm people? You know, that wants to put them turbines on my land?"

"Yes, Booger, I know."

"Well, I just found out one is that Giancarlo fella. He come out here, and he talked real rough to me. Said if I didn't hurry up and sign the papers, maybe somethin' bad would happen to the farm or to one of my boys. It makes me about sick."

"Yes, Giancarlo visited me, too. Now let's calm down and think for minute," Mrs. Entwhistle said, lowering herself into a rocker. She began moving the chair slowly back and forth. Pretty soon, Booger stopped pacing and took the other rocker, matching her easy motion. His shoulders relaxed.

"I don't know what to do," he said, but the panic was gone from his voice. "I wisht I'd never heard of no damn wind farm."

"You're under no obligation to do anything, you know," Mrs. Entwhistle said calmly, "and certainly not in a hurry. I've known Giancarlo Cicerino for years. It's not like him to act thuggish; he must be under a great deal of pressure. But we'll sort it all out, and meanwhile, you're not to worry. You just focus on your recovery."

Booger jerked his head toward the doorway where the shotgun leaned. "I reckon I can still aim pretty good if'n I have to."

Secrets and Lies

Mrs. Entwhistle was deep in thought. She pulled weeds distractedly, her mind churning with surmise. She'd heard from Butch via a brick through the window; she'd heard from Giancarlo via a threatening visit. But the person she really needed to hear from was Sissy. The wagons were being circled around her, and Mrs. Entwhistle wondered why. It was doubtful that she'd ever talk freely to Mrs. Entwhistle after their abortive interview for the newspaper, and Giancarlo was no help, swaggering around issuing threats. Time to call in reinforcements. Maxine.

Curl-E-Cue Corner was the scene of Maxine's standing weekly appointment for a wash and set. She was understandably vain about her lovely silver mane, still thick and springy. Mrs. Entwhistle stifled a pang of pure envy. But then she thought if she couldn't have hair like that, she was glad Maxine did. She waited patiently, flipping through old *People* magazines until Maxine was finished.

"C'mon, Max, I'm taking you to lunch."

"At the Busy Bee Diner?"

"Nope, at the Cora Entwhistle Cafe. I've got some ripe tomatoes for sandwiches."

"Oh, yummy! My first of the summer. Let's go."

The ladies took some time peeling and slicing the shining red tomatoes. Roger sniffed disdainfully, decided he wasn't interested in any treats that might be forthcoming from such a spread, and settled down for a nap. They constructed the sandwiches with just the right amount of salt and mayo, and Mrs. Entwhistle took a big bite, using her napkin to catch the juice that ran down her chin.

"Mmmmm! There's nothing better than a garden-ripe tomato on homemade bread," she murmured with her mouth full.

Maxine nodded with a mayonnaise-lined smile. They ate blissfully, then took their frosty glasses of iced tea out on the porch. Mrs. Entwhistle sipped a while, and then spoke.

"I've got to get to the bottom of this Sissy Smith thing. I wonder if you'd be willing to help me."

"Why, honey, of course you know I'll do whatever I can. But I don't think Sissy would tell me any secrets."

"Do you think Giancarlo might?"

"I don't know. Wouldn't he be more likely to talk to you?"

"Oh, he's already done that, right here on this porch. Actually, he threatened me if I didn't leave Sissy alone, so we're not on the best of terms."

"Why, for goodness sakes! What's got into the old goat?"

"He's scared. He said he didn't want Sissy bothered, but I saw fear in his eyes. What's he afraid of, that's what I want to know. I thought...could you sort of accidentally run into him and chat him up a bit? Maybe at the Busy Bee, buy him a cup of coffee or something? Or, better yet, at the wine bar. Get him mellowed out with a little wine? Giancarlo has always been a talker. He might let something slip."

"But I don't want him to think I'm...interested in him, and he tends to think every woman is interested."

"Plenty of them have been, apparently. No, what I thought was, you tell him you're considering a reverse mortgage and want his advice. That'll get his juices pumping, don't you think?"

They smiled, remembering the hard sell he'd tried on them at their fiftieth high-school reunion.

"Well, I'll do it for you," Maxine finally said. "But you're going to be in trouble if Giancarlo becomes a problem."

~*~

Maxine was as good as her word. A couple of days passed, but then Maxine's car swung into her driveway early one morning. She didn't bother to knock. She obviously had a lot she was itching to share. She accepted a cup of tea before settling in the kitchen chair opposite Mrs. Entwhistle.

"So I engineered a 'chance meeting' with Giancarlo downtown," she began without preamble. "I had to hang around and watch for him for a day or two. Surprised I didn't get hauled in as a suspicious character, lurking around as I was. I accosted him as soon as he parked his car and invited him to join me in Le Vin for a glass of wine. He looked surprised, but I must say he was more than ready. He mentioned he'd prefer something stronger; I told him ladies in this town didn't go into bars in the middle of the day. He had two glasses of wine in about ten minutes flat. I kept pushing the little bowl of cheese straws his way, but he was intent on that wine. Say, Cora, have you noticed how bad he looks? His color is terrible, and I think he's lost ten pounds just since he's been here, and he was thin to begin with. Something's working on that man, eating up his mind or his body. Maybe both."

Mrs. Entwhistle nodded. "I've noticed that, too. He's the very picture of a worried man. Sounds like you handled him beautifully though. You got him a little tiddly. Did that loosen his tongue?"

"I feel a bit guilty about it, honestly. I asked him if he wanted to order something to eat, but he said no, he didn't have much appetite."

"I think he eats mostly sushi and those Chinese noodles and things like that," Mrs. Entwhistle said. "You know, in California they don't eat like we do here. He's probably just starving for something fried."

"Could be. Anyway, we sat there a good while and Giancarlo got chatty."

"Did you have to endure a sermon about reverse mortgages?"

"No, he said he doesn't do that anymore. Didn't seem to want to talk about it."

"No telling what trouble he got into over that," Mrs. Entwhistle said, shaking her head.

"Right. So I kind of wound the conversation around to Booger and the wind farm, because I think that's at the bottom of all this."

"You do?" Mrs. Entwhistle blinked in surprise. She had only hoped for some information about Sissy and the Booster Club; she hadn't connected the dots to the wind farm. That Maxine was a dark horse!

"Yes, and he seemed to know a great deal about it. Quoted me all kinds of figures and statistics about energy savings and return on investment. I wish I could have taken notes because I can't remember it now, but of course I couldn't be that obvious."

"No, of course you couldn't."

"But I did ask him if he was an investor. He hemmed and hawed, but I pressed him a little bit, you know, made big eyes and talked about how he knew so much about financial matters, and he finally said he was. Then I asked if anyone else in town was in on it, and he clammed right up. I could tell he wasn't going to say one more thing about it, so I changed the subject."

Mrs. Entwhistle was on the edge of her chair. "Did he talk about Sissy?"

"He sure did. By then, he was feeling the wine. We'd moved to the patio, and it was coming on dusk; we were just sitting and rocking, looking at the lightening bugs. He said it reminded him of when he was a boy, and he got all nostalgic. We talked about high school days and the fun we had, games and pep rallies and who dated who. He talked some about Floyd and you."

"He did? What did he say?"

"That he thought you were the smartest girl he ever knew, and he wished sometimes he'd beaten Floyd's time with you."

"Huh. Like he could have." Mrs. Entwhistle tried to hide her pleasure at this validation. She'd had such a secret crush on Giancarlo back in high school, but believed she wasn't in the prom queen and sports car league. It was nice to feel appreciated, even sixty years later. And oh, thank goodness she'd stuck with Floyd!

"So, anyways, I started talking about our kids, what they were doing these days, grandkids and all that. And Giancarlo talked about Sissy. If he remembers what all he told me today, he'll be upset. It seems

Sissy and Butch are having trouble."

Mrs. Entwhistle nodded. "Butch told me. It was just like we talked about, how you can't judge by appearances what goes on in other people's marriages. I sure hope they can work it out."

She'd helped Tommy get through his divorce, and knew first-hand what an upheaval it caused, with ripple-effects right through the whole family. Tommy's children had blamed their father and thought she took his side, though she'd tried hard to be neutral. As a result, she wasn't as close to Tommy's children as she'd have liked. But she didn't hold it against them. They'd suffered, too, and time would bring them understanding. Meanwhile, she kept in touch as best she could with birthday and Christmas presents, phone calls (no matter how stilted the conversation), and invitations to come see her. Of course, when those children attained the age of twenty-five, they'd come into the nice little nest egg she'd set aside for them. It'd be enough for a down-payment on that first house, or maybe pay the tuition for a Ph.D. The thought filled her with satisfaction, although she'd probably not be around to see it. She jerked her attention back to what Max was saying.

"I asked him if he thought they'd split up. He said Sissy was just getting her ducks in a row so she could leave Butch, that she was going to move to California and live with him."

"Wow!" Mrs. Entwhistle's eyes were round. "Wonder how Butch will take that?"

"Not well, I'd guess. I've known him since he was a young'un, and he was always tenacious and stubborn. He never liked to share or give up what was his. I don't reckon he's changed much. I wonder exactly what getting ducks in a row means in Sissy's case," Maxine said.

"I have a feeling it has to do with money," Mrs. Entwhistle said. "It usually does."

Young Legs

Mrs. Entwhistle tossed and tumbled in her bed. Roger made little groaning sounds of protest when she disturbed him. Finally, she got up, put on her robe and went downstairs to watch some television. That always worked when she was trying to view a program she wanted to see. She'd drop right off in the middle of it and miss the end, which made her so mad. But not tonight. Tonight her mind kept racing around like a monkey in a tree. Mrs. Entwhistle had taken one yoga class long ago, and she knew to call what she was experiencing "monkey mind." She couldn't get the little critter to keep still and let her sleep.

Her mind whirled, a jumble of Sissy, Booster Club malfeasance, wind farms, and Booger. Finally Mrs. Entwhistle got a sheet of paper and began to organize what she knew and what she suspected. In fact, she made two columns: What I Know and What

I Suspect.

What I Know

Booster Club funds are unaccounted for; Sissy is president of the Booster Club

Sissy and Butch are having marital problems

Giancarlo has come back from California

Booger has an offer to put wind turbines on his farm

Giancarlo is an investor in that venture

What I Suspect

Sissy is stealing from Booster Club funds

Her father is up to something shady

It all has something to do with the wind farm (thanks, Max)

The act of putting her thoughts on paper finally quieted her monkey mind. With a sigh, she settled back in bed, curled up on her side and, to Roger's relief, slept.

The next morning, she awoke with a feeling of clarity. "I guess my brain was working on it while I slept," she told Roger.

Eager to discuss her thoughts with Jimmy Jack, she dressed and went to the *Pantograph* office. But at her desk in the newsroom sat a new person, someone she'd never met, which in itself was rare since she knew everyone in town. But this young person was a stranger. She studied him as he stared at the computer screen.

Very early twenties, she figured, maybe only twenty-one; hair in a trendy forward swoop on top, short on the sides. Big black horn-rimmed glasses that dwarfed his face. He was tall and skinny, and wore clothes she could only suppose were the height of style, clothes that screamed, "I'm not from around here!" Just then, he glanced up, saw her, and scrambled to his feet with an apology.

"Oh, sorry, you must be Mrs. Entwhistle," he said.

"Sometimes I'm sorry I must be Mrs. Entwhistle, too," she said with a smile, extending her hand. The young man shook it vigorously.

"I'm Dex Schofield," he said. "I didn't mean to take your desk. They just told me to sit here while they get my paperwork ready."

"Paperwork?"

"Yeah, today's my first day. I'm the new intern reporter," Dex said, trying for modesty, but failing.

"Well. Welcome. You just sit right there, I need to see Jimmy Jack anyway."

"Jimmy Jack?"

"I mean, Mr. McNamara."

Jimmy Jack's glass door stood open, so she didn't bother to knock. She took a seat across from his desk.

"I didn't know you were planning to hire a new reporter," she said.

"Sorry, I kept forgetting to tell you, what with all

that's going on," Jimmy Jack said. "I hope you don't mind sharing a desk with him."

"I don't mind a bit. I'm seldom here, anyway. Tell me about him."

Jimmy Jack obliged. Dex was a rising senior in journalism at the university. He'd applied for an internship at the *Pantograph* because he thought actual work experience, even at no pay, would give him an edge when it came time to apply for big-city jobs.

"Does he understand about the PTA meetings and ladies' teas?" Mrs. Entwhistle asked.

"I told him. He probably doesn't really understand and won't until he's covered a few."

They shared a rueful smile. Jimmy Jack continued. Dex would be with them for the summer and during that time, he hoped Mrs. Entwhistle would serve as his mentor.

"That's assuming I know what I'm doing," she said, "and that's a big assumption."

"Seriously, Mrs. Entwhistle, I'll feel better if you just let Dex follow you around. You'll be safer, and you'll have young legs to run errands. I worry about you."

"That's mighty sweet of you, honey," Mrs. Entwhistle said, forgetting that she'd resolved to call him Mr. McNamara in the office. "But I feel perfectly safe. My goodness, I've lived here all my life."

"Still, if you wouldn't mind, I'd appreciate it if you'd look after Dex. And maybe let him look after you, too."

~*~

"And Dex is short for...what?" Mrs. Entwhistle asked, watching the young man down a donut in three bites.

"Dexter. The kids called me Poindexter in school. I had to win a few fights to earn being just Dex."

"I don't need a bloody nose to convince me to call you just Dex. Now, what do you want to do today?"

Mrs. Entwhistle had carried Dex to the Busy Bee for a get-acquainted second breakfast, and their conversation had been easy and unforced. Dex was a delightful youngster, Mrs. Entwhistle thought, charmingly deferential, yet with a wicked twinkle in his eye. She admitted to herself that she had a soft spot for rascals, and Dex clearly was one.

"Whatever *you're* doing, that's what I'd like to do today," he said now, grinning at her.

"Well, the Friends of the Library are meeting at two; at four there's a planning meeting for the First Methodist Church's annual fund-raiser. I need to cover those two events. But this morning, I'd like to just introduce you around, get you acquainted with the town."

Dex's face lit up. "Can't think of anything I'd like better."

Mrs. Entwhistle walked him up one side of Main Street and down the other. He met Floyd the barber ("Yes, just like on the 'Andy Griffith' show.") He said hello to the ladies in the Curl-E-Cue, with a special smile for Ronnie Sue. Mrs. Entwhistle had to warn him later that Ronnie Sue was engaged and definitely off the market. They stopped at Ed's Chevron, but Ed was too busy to do more than wave. Then she took him by her house to meet Roger. Dex immediately dropped to the floor beside the old dog and gently scratched him under the chin. Roger's filmy eyes blinked in pleasure, and he bestowed several licks on Dex's arm. Mrs. Entwhistle believed that dogs can tell good people from bad, so Dex rose in her opinion.

They'd only just met, but because she trusted her instincts and Roger's, and because they were, after all, fellow reporters, Mrs. Entwhistle decided to take Dex into her confidence. She told him about Sissy and Butch and Booger and the wind farm and the brick through the window. It took a while to tell it all, and meanwhile she and Dex shared a soup and sandwich lunch. He was no different than Tommy'd been at that age: an abyss of hunger, always waiting to be refilled. She ladled out big bowls of Maxine's special potato soup to go with the sandwiches, and finished by cutting him a huge slice of gingerbread piled with whipped cream. He listened intently, so absorbed in her story that he didn't notice what he was eating, but shoveled it in anyway like the boy he was. Mrs. Entwhistle's heart warmed.

"So, what are you going to do?" he asked when she was finished with her tale.

"I thought the next thing would be to talk to Booger

again. I don't want him worried by the turbine people; he's just getting over a heart attack. He got a stent, you know."

"Yeah, my grandpa had to get one, too, and he did just fine. I'd sure like to meet this Booger person and see his place. Does he have a real name?"

"Everyone's called him Booger since first grade. I doubt he'd answer to anything else. Look, one thing I haven't mentioned. Jimmy Jack, I mean, Mr. McNamara doesn't like for me to dig into all this stuff. He said I'm to stick to teas and business meetings, but I just can't let this go. Maybe you'll get in trouble with him if you help me."

"Well, bring it on then, Mrs. E.! I wouldn't miss this for anything."

Mrs. Entwhistle wasn't sure she liked being addressed as Mrs. E., but she didn't say anything. They walked out to the driveway and surveyed their transportation options.

Dex got around on a little scooter. That clearly wouldn't do, so she tossed him her car keys. He drove at a considerably higher rate of speed than she was used to. Mrs. Entwhistle's right foot hit an imaginary brake several times, but she reminded herself that Floyd always said it was good for a car to be driven fast sometimes – blew the carbon out of the engine, or something like that. She closed her eyes and when she opened them again, they were at Booger's place, and she was still alive and all in one piece. Her legs quit shaking after she'd walked a few steps.

Repeated knocks on the door brought no answer. Mrs. Entwhistle would have gone away, thinking Caleb had taken his father to a doctor's appointment or something. But Dex was curious. He roamed around the grounds, following a swath of crushed grass to an outbuilding at the far end of the yard.

"Mrs. E, come here, quick!" Dex's voice sounded urgent.

She hurried to where he stood in the open door of the tool shed. On the dirt floor lay Booger, looking strangely small for such a large man. He'd been beaten, and his beard was stained red with blood running from a cut on his forehead. Dex knelt by the old man's side and felt for a pulse in his neck.

"Fast and faint, but still beating," he said briefly. "Call 911."

Mrs. Entwhistle's fingers were numb with shock as she fumbled in her purse for her cell phone. "Linda, it's Cora Entwhistle. I'm at Booger's place, he needs an ambulance real quick. No, he's alive, but unconscious. Looks like somebody beat him."

The ambulance seemed to take forever, but in reality, it was only ten minutes before the EMTs were gently lifting Mrs. Entwhistle from where she sat beside Booger on the dirt floor of the shed. She'd held his bloody hand in hers, talking to him in a conversational way. Occasionally, Booger would groan and flutter his eyes, so she thought he could hear her.

"Now, Booger, you're going to be all right. You got a

knock on the head, that's all, and with that hard head of yours, why, you probably didn't even feel it. You'll be back on your feet in no time, you just wait and see."

When the paramedics went to work, Dex led her to the front porch and sat her in a rocking chair. She watched as the stretcher bump over the grass to the open maw of the ambulance. Then, heralded by red lights and siren, Booger was on his way to the hospital. She felt like she was watching something on television, and wished she could change the channel. Dex came and sat down beside her. They rocked silently for a few minutes.

"Any idea why someone would beat up an old man?" he finally asked.

"No idea who, but some idea why. Something to do with the wind farm, would be my guess. I don't know if Booger had signed the lease agreement yet, what with his heart attack and all. I think he intended to, but maybe hadn't gotten around to it yet."

A battered pickup truck ground its way up the drive. Caleb emerged from the cab and came toward them with a question on his face. "Mrs. Entwhistle? Why are you here? Where's Dad?"

"Now, Caleb, don't panic, honey. Your dad's been taken to the hospital," she said.

"Hospital? Did he have another heart attack?"

"No, or at least I don't think he did. Somebody beat him up. We found him."

"You and who?" Caleb asked, looking at Dex.

"Dex Schofield," Dex said, sticking out his hand to Caleb. "I'm working with Mrs. Entwhistle."

Caleb shook the offered hand dazedly. "But who... Why... Is Dad going to be okay?"

"I'm sure he will be," Mrs. Entwhistle said. She was not sure at all, but felt it was important to keep Caleb calm. "I think we should all head to the hospital now. Do you want to ride with us?"

"No, I better drive. Don't know when I'll be able to leave," Caleb said. "I've got to call Nate." He reached for his cell and punched in numbers. "Go on ahead, I'm right behind you."

At the hospital, the three of them alternately sat or paced in the hospital waiting room. That space had been vastly improved since the old days of uncomfortable chairs and old magazines. Now a coffee bar offered drinks and snacks, and several copies of the day's *Pantograph* were strewn on table tops. But waiting for news hadn't changed; it was still a time fraught with worry and tension.

Mrs. Entwhistle recognized the doctor the minute he came in the door, despite his official white coat and stethoscope. "Why, Brownie, how are you?" she asked.

For it was little John Brown Hochner, always known as "Brownie" after his mother's people. Mrs. Entwhistle had known him since he was on the Cradle Roll at church, a nice, studious boy with a talent for science. Now he was the doctor attending poor Booger. Mrs. Entwhistle was glad to see him, but wished he didn't look like a twelve-year-old playing dress-up.

"Mrs. Entwhistle, Caleb," Dr. Hochner said, raising an inquisitive eyebrow in Dex's direction.

"This is Dex Schofield, new intern at the *Pantograph*; Dex, meet Dr. Brownie Hochner," Mrs. Entwhistle said. "And now tell us about Booger. Is he going to be all right?"

"He has a concussion and some nasty bruises. I had to stitch the gash in his forehead; that blow was probably what gave him the concussion. His chest will hurt the worst because there's a fractured rib, but I think everything will heal. He is elderly, so things can sometimes take a bad turn, but I feel optimistic. What happened to him? It wasn't on his chart. Car accident?"

"No, he got a beat-down," Caleb said.

At that moment his brother, Nate, threw open the door with a crash. "Where's Dad?" he demanded, wild-eyed. "Is he gonna make it? What bastard did this to him? I'll kill him, I swear I'll kill him." He looked around for someone to punch.

Mrs. Entwhistle stepped forward. "Your father is going to be all right, Nate. Take some deep breaths now and see if you can slow down a little bit. I know you hurried to get here, and of course you're upset, who wouldn't be? Sit here, won't you? Now just breathe in and out for a minute. Caleb, would you get your brother a cup of coffee?"

Gradually, Nate's breathing slowed. His hand shook as he took the proffered coffee cup, but he managed to take a few sips without spilling. Mrs. Entwhistle sat beside him with her hand on his shoulder.

"Now, then," she said, "that's better. Remember Brownie? He was a year or so ahead of you in school, and now he's your dad's doctor. Isn't that something? Brownie, tell Nate what you just told us."

~*~

By the time Dex pulled into Mrs. Entwhistle's driveway, night had fallen and she was exhausted. "Oh, law, I'm too old for this," she moaned. "And we completely missed the Friends of the Library and the First Methodist Church. But I need to drop you off at your place. I don't want you to ride that scooter after dark."

"Please don't worry about me," Dex said, taking her house key and unlocking the door for her. "You go on in and sit down. Come on, Roger, let's go out."

When they came back inside, Roger prancing a little in excitement at having a new escort, Dex headed into the kitchen and filled the dog's bowl with kibble. "Now," he said, "Roger's taken care of. Can I get you anything? Some iced tea? Or a bite to eat?"

"No, thank you so much, honey, I'm fine. Let me take you home."

"No, ma'am, I'm going to be real careful on my scooter. It has a good, strong headlight and tail lights, too, and I'll put on my reflective safety vest. I'll be perfectly all right; I ride in the dark all the time. I'll see you tomorrow at the *Pantograph*."

And with that, he was gone. Mrs. Entwhistle sighed with relief at being left alone to regroup. She couldn't remember when she'd felt so bone-weary. Her legs ached from hips to toes, like she'd been running, although it had been a long time since she'd run anywhere. Having a strong youngster taking over for a few minutes had been lovely. Maybe Jimmy Jack had been right. Poor old Booger, first a heart attack, and now this. What was this town coming to, such goings on... Tomorrow maybe she'd get her cane out again, even if it did make her look old... She'd just close her eyes for a couple of minutes.

Mrs. Entwhistle, Private Eye

Dex looked impossibly bright-eyed when Mrs. Entwhistle dragged herself into the *Pantograph* office the next morning. It didn't help that she'd slept the whole night on the couch where she'd dropped when he'd brought her home. She'd awakened at five a.m. feeling like road kill, but a hot shower and a big breakfast brought her to life again. They also made her late, something she deplored in other people and was embarrassed by in herself. Not that Dex seemed to notice. Mrs. Entwhistle had observed that the young were casual about time, and this morning she was glad of it.

"Let's visit Booger in the hospital," Dex began. "and see if he can tell us who beat him up."

Mrs. Entwhistle cast a nervous glance at Jimmy Jack's door, but Dex said, "No worries, Mr. McNamara called in sick this morning."

He flashed her a conspiratorial grin, and they headed for the door like two teenagers skipping school. Mrs. Entwhistle eyed Dex's scooter speculatively, but in the end, she drove them in her car. On the way, they formulated a plan.

~*~

Booger couldn't remember a thing. He looked anxiously at Caleb when Mrs. Entwhistle asked how he was feeling. Caleb answered for him.

"He said he's got a pretty bad headache this morning, and his rib hurts."

"No wonder," Mrs. Entwhistle said. "Booger, I'm not going to trouble you very much, but I just wondered if you remember who hit you."

"Did somebody hit me?" the old man asked wonderingly. "I thought I just fell down in the shed."

"No, Dad, you got beat up," Caleb said. "Remember, I told you that earlier."

"Oh, yeah," Booger said, squinting at his son. "I 'member now."

But it was clear he didn't. Mrs. Entwhistle and Dex exchanged glances, she nodded slightly, and Dex asked Caleb if he'd step into the hall with them for a moment. Time for Plan B.

"Look, your dad is obviously not up for questioning right now," he said. "Do you mind if we go out to his place and nose around a little?"

"I don't mind, but the cops will probably beat you to

it. Nate called them last night and reported what happened to Dad."

"That was the right thing to do," Mrs. Entwhistle said. "We'll stay out of the way of an investigation."

They were relieved to see no police cars at Booger's farm when they arrived. Local law enforcement consisted only of the sheriff and a couple of deputies. Apparently, they hadn't made it to Booger's place yet. Probably too busy with speeders and jay-walkers, Mrs. Entwhistle thought uncharitably.

She'd had a phone conversation with Pete Peters during the drive to get some tips on what to look for.

"Be alert for footprints in soft ground and be careful not to walk over them," Pete said, "and try not to touch anything. Wear gloves. If you find what you think might have been used in the attack, take a picture, but leave it right where it is. Don't pick anything up or move anything."

"Well, Pete, that's more what not to do than what to do."

"Exactly. You want to keep the crime scene untouched for law enforcement."

Mrs. Entwhistle wondered if Sheriff Trevino knew how to conduct an investigation like the one called for here. He mostly ran in the occasional drunk driver and supplied deputies for the courthouse. But Pete was right, they surely didn't want to make things any tougher for law enforcement. She told Dex they'd better wear gloves. She had some thin plastic ones she used when she pulled weeds, and she'd brought them both a pair.

They poked around the house and outbuildings, but found nothing suspicious, at least not to their untrained eyes. Mrs. Entwhistle noticed a few threads stuck to the splintery door jamb of the shed, and Dex dutifully snapped a photo of them with his phone. Dex thought he could smell a lingering scent of aftershave that might have been worn by the intruder, but it turned out to be a bushel of overripe pears.

They did notice one thing out of place. Booger's shotgun was laying on the porch floor. Mrs. Entwhistle knew he always kept it just inside the door.

"Lookie there," she said, "I believe Booger had his shotgun out when whoever it was got ahold of him. Do you think that's a clue?"

"I do," Dex said solemnly. "I bet Booger didn't like the looks of whoever came to his door, so he got his gun."

"Why didn't he shoot him, I wonder?"

"He's an old man," Dex began, then stopped, seeing the look on Mrs. Entwhistle's face. "I mean, maybe the other guy was just too fast for him, took him by surprise and knocked the gun out of his hands."

"Why did they drag him out to the shed?"

"I don't know. Hope Booger can remember what happened after he gets better."

Mrs. Entwhistle looked at the house speculatively. "What I'd like to see is the agreement with Winterberry Wind Farms. Did Booger ever sign it? If he didn't, is that why he got beat up? Had he changed his mind, and was somebody trying to force him to change it back? And what's the all-fired big deal about a bunch of turbines on a little old farm? Why would they be that important? There's more here than we're seeing, Dex."

~*~

"I still don't think this is a good idea," Mrs. Entwhistle said, casting nervous glances into the corners of the farmyard.

Dex had convinced her to return to Booger's place after dark. His reasoning was that whoever beat Booger up might return to continue their search, knowing there was no one home because the family was at the hospital.

"I'm betting he'll come back and try to find that agreement," Dex said. "If we get there first and hide, we'll see who it is. We won't do anything to apprehend him, but we can give the police a description."

"I don't know," Mrs. Entwhistle said. "We'd be trespassing, so maybe whatever we said wouldn't count."

"No, you're thinking of entrapment, like on crime shows. We won't be doing anything like that; we'll just be observers. Besides, we got permission from Caleb to be here."

Noting her dubious face, Dex said, "Hey, I can go alone. Maybe it's too much for a lady of your...station in life."

She knew he'd been about to say "a lady of your age," and as usual, being reminded of her years put her back up. While she felt perfectly free to play the age card when it suited her, nobody else had better.

"No, I'll come," she said, chin in the air. "You don't know everyone in town yet, but if it's a local person, I'll recognize him. Besides, your mama wouldn't want you out there in the dark alone."

Dex nodded meekly, suppressing a smile. And so the pair found themselves creeping through the tall grass in back of Booger's tool shed that night. Both were dressed in dark clothes and plastic gloves, and Mrs. Entwhistle had covered her white hair with a scarf. Dex proposed putting camouflage paint on their faces, but she drew the line at that.

Silently, they slipped inside the tool shed, leaving the door open a couple of inches. "Do you think this is the best vantage point?" Mrs. Entwhistle whispered.

"Not really. I can't see a thing. I'd actually rather be in the house," Dex whispered back. "Anybody searching for a document would look there, not out here in the yard. Are you game to try to get inside?"

Of course, when he put it that way, she was. "But not if we have to break in," she stipulated. "Booger never locks his doors, but Caleb might've. I won't break in, you understand?"

Dex nodded and ran to try the front door, which was firmly locked. He tried the back door – also locked. Mrs. Entwhistle joined him as he stood staring at the house in frustration.

"Booger used to have a dog that lived in the house with him," Mrs. Entwhistle said. "I bet you there's a doggie door."

And sure enough, just beside the back door was a small, square hole covered by a plastic flap. When Mrs. Entwhistle pushed the flap with her foot, it swung in easily. The little door measured about twelve by nineteen inches.

"I don't think this would count as a break-in, do you?" Mrs. Entwhistle said. "Caleb said we could look around, and we're not breaking anything."

Dex looked at the tiny door; he looked at her; his face was a study of indecision.

"I think I can get through it," he said, "but..."

Before he could finish, Mrs. Entwhistle got down on her hands and knees and stuck her head through the opening. She wiggled through until her shoulders got caught, then backed out.

"Mrs. E., I really don't think..." Dex sputtered, but she didn't stop to listen.

She tried again, this time stretched full-length on her side, arms extended over her head. She began squirming her way into Booger's kitchen, inch by inch. She could hear Dex talking, but so intent was she on her mission that she paid no attention. When she was inside up to her waist, her lower body got stuck. Shimmy and wiggle as she might, she didn't budge. And what was worse, when she tried to back out, she couldn't. She was stuck in a dog door, in the middle of the night, in the middle of somebody else's house, and who knew what nefarious characters might be lurking about.

Claustrophobia flickered across her mind, but she would not give in to panic. She lay still for a minute, glad she'd worn a pair of Floyd's old pants for this excursion. The view Dex had from outside the dog door didn't bear thinking about.

As her eyes adjusted to the dark, she saw that if she twisted at the waist and reached up, she could just grasp the kitchen door knob. She said a silent thank-you for her long arms, gave the doorknob a tentative twirl, and sure enough, the door was locked only with a push button in the middle of the knob. It swung open to reveal Dex's astonished face looking down at her where she lay half-in, half-out of Booger's dog-door.

"I could've done that, I've been saying I could crawl through and open the door for you, I tried to tell you, but...."

"Come on in here now and see if you can help me get through the rest of the way," she said.

It took some pulling, with Dex grabbing her under the arms and bracing his feet on the wall. There was an ominous ripping sound from somewhere about her person, but she finally slid the rest of the way into the kitchen. She got to her feet with Dex's help and brushed off her clothing, inspecting a long tear in the leg of Floyd's pants. Since it didn't affect modesty, she decided to ignore it.

"I'll feel that little escapade tomorrow," she said. "Yuck! Booger's kitchen floor isn't the most hygienic place to get stuck."

Dex seemed unable to speak. His face was working strangely, and he kept biting his lip. Mrs. Entwhistle thought he might be going to cry.

"Now, now," she said, patting his arm.

He turned away with a sort of coughing fit, shoulders shaking. Finally, he wiped his hand over his face and regained his composure.

The only light in the kitchen came from the illuminated clock on the stove so Mrs. Entwhistle couldn't see him very well, but she thought he had tears in his eyes. She hoped their adventure wasn't proving to be too much for him.

Well, bless his heart, he's just a young'un, it's exciting for him, she thought. She patted his arm reassuringly. "Don't be afraid, I'm right here," she said.

Dex had another coughing fit, pulled out his handkerchief and blew his nose. Then he settled himself and said, "Okay, what do you think we should do next?"

At that moment, they both heard the sound of a car approaching. "Quick, hide!" Mrs. Entwhistle said, her eyes scanning the dim kitchen for a likely place.

Dex darted to a door and flung it open to total blackness. "Basement! C'mon."

They didn't dare shine even the tiny pen lights they'd brought until the door closed behind them. Groping along the wall and hanging on to each other, they trained the lights on their feet and descended step by step. They took a quick look around to get their bearings, found the darkest corner and crouched there.

The basement was really more of a cellar, low, earthen-floored and dank. Dex couldn't stand upright and the top of Mrs. Entwhistle's head brushed the dirty rafters. Thinking of the spiders that certainly lived there, she was glad she'd worn a scarf over her hair.

They listened in breathless silence and heard the tinkle of broken glass. A door in need of some oil in the hinges creaked open. Heavy footsteps thudded above them, followed by light that seeped through cracks in the floor. Mrs. Entwhistle thought Booger really needed to put in new insulation. It must be hard to heat the house with all those chinks. For what seemed like an eternity, they crouched barely daring to breathe. Above them, papers crinkled and objects were flung to the floor with a crash. Mrs. Entwhistle got a painful cramp in her back that she didn't dare stretch to alleviate. She and Dex listened as the intruderss moving from room to room, and she could only give thanks that Booger's house was small. Searching it wouldn't take long.

When the cellar door opened and they heard the

intruder groping along the wall for a light switch, Mrs. Entwhistle's heart thudded. If there was an overhead light, they were doomed. But luckily, Booger had never wired the cellar for electricity. A flashlight swept the stairs, but didn't reach the dark corner where they hid. After a moment, they heard, "Ain't nothin' down there," and the door swing shut again. Mrs. Entwhistle's legs felt so weak she had to grope behind her for a place to sit. She realized she was clutching Dex's hand in a death grip and let go. He patted her this time. They listened as the creaky door opened and shut, the car's engine started, and tires crunched away down the gravel drive.

"It's safe now. Let's go back upstairs," Dex said in a normal voice that sounded like shouting.

But first, Mrs. Entwhistle switched on her little light and shone it methodically around the underground room. There was a big, old, oil-burning furnace with a rusty tank hulking beside it. Crates and pallets and boxes and barrels lined the walls. Mice scurried away from the light. Mrs. Entwhistle shivered, but she was determined to look around since she was here anyway. Dex followed her lead, shining his light around the walls and floors.

"Wait, do you see what I see?" she asked. The narrow beam of her flashlight illuminated footprints on the dusty floor.

"We didn't make those prints," Dex said.

Careful where he stepped, he followed them to a rickety open cupboard that contained ancient Mason jars full of dark fruit.

"Wouldn't want to eat those peaches," Mrs. Entwhistle murmured.

Among the glass jars they saw the corner of a brown envelope. Dex eased it out from its hiding place and shone his light on it.

"Winterberry Wind Farms," he read.

Just Like Nancy Drew

"I'm telling you, Max, it was just like a Nancy Drew book. You remember, when you're screaming, 'Nancy, don't go down into the basement! Don't go down there!' but she does it anyway. That was Dex and me."

Maxine's eyes were huge. "Cora, you could have broken a hip!" she said.

"Breaking a hip was the least of my worries," Mrs. Entwhistle replied. "If whoever broke in Booger's house had caught us, I don't know what they'd have done to us."

"You were so brave!" Maxine breathed. "I never would have been able to do it."

"Of course you would," Mrs. Entwhistle said, smiling at her friend. "You're brave as a lion when you need to be. So, anyway, after they left, Dex and I investigated the cellar, and we found this."

She brandished the brown envelope. She and Dex had already made themselves familiar with the contents. It was the Winterberry Wind Farms agreement, all right, with Booger's shaky signature on the bottom line. She smoothed the document out on Maxine's kitchen table, taking care not to get blueberry muffin crumbs on it. Maxine adjusted her trifocals so she could get a good look.

"We think Booger must have had misgivings after he signed," Mrs. Entwhistle said, "and hid the documents while he had another think about it. Then somebody came and demanded the paperwork. Well, you know Booger. You don't demand anything from him. He must have gotten his shotgun from beside the front door, because it was laying on the porch right outside."

"Then what happened?"

"We don't know for sure, but we think that's when Booger got beat up. I could have told whoever beat him that it was useless. That old man just doubles down when he's cornered. I expect he'd have died rather than give in."

"Well, my stars." Maxine was at a loss for words. Accustomed as she was to her friend's intrepidity, this adventure left her speechless. She got up and carried their bowls to the stove, where she ladled out more of her homemade cheese soup.

"Not too much," Mrs. Entwhistle cautioned. She'd already had a big bowl.

"Just half a ladle," Maxine put the bowls on the table. "You need to keep up your strength if you're going to be up to such shenanigans. Although I don't want to fatten you up so you can't get through doggie doors."

They laughed and Mrs. Entwhistle said, "Good thing I'm tall and skinny, but even so, poor Dex had a time getting me all the way through. I ripped Floyd's pants."

"He doesn't need them anymore."

"Oh, my, Max, what do you think Floyd would say if he knew about this?"

"Why, I expect he'd say, 'Something smells fishy, Cora, you let me handle it.'"

They smiled pensively. They missed their old-fashioned, chivalrous husbands.

Mrs. Entwhistle and Dex sat on her porch trying to figure out what to do next. They agreed it was better if they didn't have their discussions in the *Pantograph* office, since neither had breathed a word about their adventure to Jimmy Jack.

They had some good theories about what had happened, but hard evidence was proving elusive. Repeated attempts to jog Booger's memory had been unsuccessful. Dr. Hochner said he might never recall the period of time around the attack. All Caleb knew was that his father was talking to some unspecified people about placing wind turbines on his land; that was it, he couldn't add anything more.

Nate hadn't even known that much. Both sons agreed that whatever their dad did with his land was up to him. Mrs. Entwhistle thought their lack of greed for their inheritance was refreshing, but wished they'd paid more attention to their father.

"I think the next person to talk to is Giancarlo Cicerino," Mrs. Entwhistle said. "He's got to be mixed up in all this somehow."

"You've known him all your life, right?" Dex said. "Will he open up to you?"

"Yes, I've known Giancarlo since we were kids, but whether he'll tell me anything is another matter. He's turned into a skunky low-life in his old age. Remember, I told you he actually came around and told me to leave Sissy alone or else. We're not on the best of terms. Maxine got more information out of him than I could've, and she had to get him tipsy."

"How are you going to get around that?"

"I'll break out my secret weapon."

Giancarlo didn't hide his surprise at hearing from her, and he was even more surprised to be invited to supper. He hemmed and hawed on the verge of refusing, so Mrs. Entwhistle played her ace.

"Fried green tomatoes," she said. "For old times' sake."

"I'll be there," he replied, as she'd known he would. Somebody who'd spent his adult life in California eating raw fish wouldn't be able to pass up fried green tomatoes.

He ate country-fried steak, mashed potatoes with gravy, fried green tomatoes, and fresh green beans cooked with bacon as though he hadn't eaten in months. For a skinny fellow, he packed it away. When Mrs. Entwhistle brought out the pecan pie, he actually groaned.

"I don't think I can..." he said.

She cut him a piece and placed it in front of him. He eyed it for a minute, picked up his fork and took a bite. Then another. Then the plate was empty. With glassy eyes, he followed her to the porch and eased down in a rocking chair. She set his iced tea on the table beside him and sat down herself. So far, her strategy was working. Giancarlo looked stunned and malleable.

"Wow, that was some meal," he said, loosening his belt. "You could kill a guy with that kind of cooking."

"I don't cook big meals much since Floyd passed," Mrs. Entwhistle confessed. "It seems silly to go to so much trouble just for myself. It was a pleasure to feed you, Giancarlo."

"Just call me Carlo," he said, "everyone in CA does."

"Well, we're not in CA, and you'll always be Giancarlo to me. Why did you come home, anyway? You've been out there on the West Coast for years. Why home; why now?"

"Sissy asked me to come," he said. "She said she needed me. I haven't been much of a father to her –

or to my other kids, either – so I thought it was a chance to try to make it up to her."

"What's the matter with Sissy?" Mrs. Entwhistle asked bluntly.

"She wants to divorce Butch and move to California and live with me," Giancarlo said, looking glum. "I keep trying to tell her it's maybe not such a good idea, but she's got her mind set. I don't know what Estelle will say if I show up with a middle-aged daughter."

Mrs. Entwhistle guessed Estelle must be the latest wife. She'd lost count of how many there'd been. One thing you could say about Giancarlo, he married 'em. For a while.

"Sissy hasn't been herself lately, I've noticed that." Mrs. Entwhistle decided to lay her cards on the table. "I think she's done something wrong with the Booster Club funds."

He gazed at her unhappily. "If you've figured that out, everyone else will soon enough."

It wasn't exactly flattering, but it was true. The anonymous items in the "Palaver" testified to the fact that someone was hot on Sissy's trail. That probably explained her sudden urge to move to California.

Giancarlo burped discreetly. "She wants me to cut her in on a little investment I'm working on. It's a sure thing; she could replace the Booster Club money and have a nice little nest egg."

"Are you going to do it?"

"It's not entirely up to me. I've got partners, other investors, who don't want to let anyone else in. I'm trying to change their minds, but it's not going well, and Sissy is driving me crazy. She's scared to death she's going to get caught."

"Why did she take the money in the first place?"

"She needs it to finance a divorce, is what she told me," Giancarlo said with a sigh. "I tried to tell her divorce isn't all it's cracked up to be."

Mrs. Entwhistle stifled a snort and merely nodded. She didn't want him to stop talking.

"But she says she's done with Butch and wants to get as far away from him as possible, so she decided to 'borrow' from the Booster Club. That's what she calls it, borrowing. The thing is, Sissy can't handle money. She's taken more than enough to finance a divorce and a move, but she's spent most of it on other stuff. Now she doesn't have enough to leave, and she's afraid she'll be arrested if she stays. That's why she wants in on my investment opportunity."

"How much has she taken, exactly?"

"I don't think even she knows without an audit, but enough for it to be a felony. If she gets caught, she'll go to jail. This is one time in her life when she can't expect good old Butch to bail her out, since getting rid of him is her motivation. I wish I could help her, but I don't have a lot of savings, and I've got ex-wives and other kids in line in front of her. And there's no time...."

Mrs. Entwhistle's ears perked up. "What do you mean, no time?"

There was a long pause. Giancarlo picked up his tea and sipped. At last, he turned to look her in the eye. "I'm dying, Cora. I've got pancreatic cancer. That's why I'm so skinny and yellow."

Mrs. Entwhistle wasn't totally surprised - she'd had her suspicions - but she was sympathetic. "Oh, Giancarlo, I'm sorry. How long have you known?"

"About six months. I had some treatments, but they were so awful I decided to let nature take its course. I'm tired, ready to be done with it all."

"But yet you came back for Sissy."

"I'm not much good to her, I'm afraid."

"She'll never forget that you came, though. That's what counts. I'm as sorry as I can be to hear your news, but I respect your decision to stop treatment. It's pretty rough, and we die anyway, don't we? If you choose to spend your last days as you wish, I can't blame you. What can I do to help?"

"Thanks, Cora. There's not much you can do for me, but do you think you could talk some sense into Sissy?"

"I tried to talk to her, and to Butch, too. She wasn't having it. Neither was Butch. In fact, he threw a brick through my window."

"Yeah, I heard about the brick. Don't know what got into Butch. He must be out of his mind with worry. He doesn't know everything that Sissy's been up to, but he suspects. Maybe if you tried talking to her as a friend, not as a reporter...."

"But I *am* a reporter now, Giancarlo. I owe it to Jimmy Jack to do my job. It looks like you, Sissy, Booger and the Winterberry Wind Farm venture are all connected. You've said you're an investor; who are the others?"

Giancarlo sent her a sharp look, jolted out of his sated stupor He wasn't as groggy as Mrs. Entwhistle had hoped. "Why do you ask?"

"Booger's still in the hospital after that beating he took. He could have died. I don't believe you'd do anything like that, but I want to know who did it and why."

"What makes you think I'd know?"

Because you're in it up to your ears, Mrs. Entwhistle thought, but she said, "Just a hunch."

Giancarlo gazed across the green apron of grass, watching the goldfinches flitting among the zinnias. She thought he wasn't going to answer, but then he spoke.

"The Winterberry Wind Farm people are not the kind of folks Booger's used to dealing with. He can't change his mind once he's made a commitment and scare them off with his shotgun."

"But what's the big deal? If they don't get Booger's land they'll surely be able to find someplace else."

"It's more than...what meets the eye," Giancarlo said reluctantly. "You don't want to get mixed up in it,

Cora. Please believe me. And now, I really have to go."

She helped him as he struggled up from his chair, feeling how thin his arm was. She could almost close her hand around it. Suddenly, she was swept with pity. She'd had a crush on him when she was young and impressionable. It was the luckiest break of her life that she'd married Floyd instead, because look how things turned out. Still, she felt compassion for him. Despite his many wives and offspring, he was a lonely, sick old man sitting in God's waiting room listening for his name to be called.

The Slippery Slope

Dex's head was bent toward his computer screen with an intensity that suggested total concentration. Mrs. Entwhistle carefully skirted around her desk, which was at the moment his desk, so as not to disturb him. She found a chair, picked up the day's issue of the *Pantograph* and settled down to wait for Dex to finish what he was doing.

There were the usual items about town activities. The Rosemary and Thyme book club's meeting was devoted to a tome called **The Language of Flowers**, which seemed like a good fit. She and Dex had covered that. The police roster included such dangerous criminals as speeders and passers of school buses after the safety arm was lowered. There were a couple of drunk-and-disorderlies, and a man cited for animal cruelty for keeping his beagle chained in the back yard.

Mrs. Entwhistle flipped through the front page news

and went to the "Palaver" column. She'd put it together, but was still curious to see how it looked in print. The items there were much more personal.

"J.J., I miss you and love you. Please come home."

"Anybody want a swing set? Yours for the taking, our kids are all grown."

"It's not deer hunting season, so quit firing your gun in the woods behind my house. If you shoot my dog, I'll shoot you."

And then the one that had puzzled her so much she'd nearly not printed it. *"Splish splash, money's taking a bath."* What could it mean? In the end, she'd decided to include it in the column just to see if it drew a reaction.

Dex lifted his head, saw her sitting there and jumped to his feet. "Oh, sorry, Mrs. E., I didn't hear you come in. Here's your chair, I just got it warmed up for you."

The thought of sitting in a chair toasty from someone else's backside did not appeal to Mrs. Entwhistle. "No, no, stay where you are. You looked like you were deep into something."

"I was doing some Internet research," Dex said. "What do you know about money laundering?"

Every head in the newsroom (there were only two others besides theirs) came up. Dex glanced around and pulled his chair closer to Mrs. Entwhistle's.

"Why, I don't know much about it," Mrs. Entwhistle confessed. "I guess it means ill-gotten gains are funneled through legitimate channels to obscure their origins. Is that right?"

"Yeah, that's about it. It's really complicated, though. See, if a large amount of money just kind of came out of nowhere, authorities would spot it and start investigating, and you'd have to prove that you got it legally. Banks have to report deposits of more than ten thousand dollars, for example. So, if you had, say, a million dollars of dirty money from drugs or whatever, you couldn't use it until the money looked like it came from a legitimate source. You'd need to 'clean' it."

"How is that done?"

"Lots of different ways. The bad guys might invest in cash intensive businesses, like casinos or strip clubs, and then juggle the books. They might physically smuggle the cash to an off-shore bank, but that's not easy because cash is bulky. Or they might buy into or start a legitimate business, inflate the real profits with dirty money, or use the business' bank accounts as shelters."

They looked at each other for a long moment. "Splish splash, money's taking a bath," Mrs. Entwhistle said meditatively.

"Exactly."

Then, together: "Winterberry Wind Farm."

"We have to tell Jimmy Jack," Mrs. Entwhistle said.

~*~

The young editor was not pleased to be made privy

to their suspicions. He held his head in his hands and groaned.

"Why me? Why does it have to happen on my watch? My dad would have been on it like white on rice, but oh, no, it has to break while I'm in charge. All I want is a nice, quiet day."

Jimmy Jack definitely lacked a reporter's proverbial nose for news, Mrs. Entwhistle thought.

"Mr. McNamara, this is a big story for any newspaper, let alone a small-town one," she said. "You're right, your father would have been delighted, but I understand that you're relatively new to the business. Well, we three in this room all are." She looked at Dex's face, lit by excitement, and Jimmy Jack's, a study of gloom. "But we have an obligation to pursue it, don't you think?"

"I don't even know how to begin." Jimmy Jack was tugging at his hair now. "Couldn't we just report it to the sheriff..." His voice trailed off. They all knew the sheriff was not equipped to deal with a problem of this magnitude.

"I know a Deputy U.S. Marshall," Mrs. Entwhistle said, "and he's just the man to consult. Pete Peters will know what to do."

"But meanwhile, we can be gathering evidence," Dex said. His legs jiggled with the effort of keeping from running out of his editor's office and beginning the chase.

~*~

"This is Pulitzer material!" he told Mrs. Entwhistle later.

"Whoa, let's not get ahead of our skis," Mrs. Entwhistle said. She'd heard her son, Tommy, use that expression and thought it painted a perfect mental picture of someone going downhill too fast, arms flailing. "We need to talk to Pete."

But Pete wasn't home. His wife, Sheila, said he was out of town on a case, and she didn't expect him back for two weeks. He was on the West Coast, she added while trying to discourage her children from completely swamping Mrs. Entwhistle, whom they considered fair game as their honorary grandma.

Mrs. Entwhistle untangled herself from the scrum of little boys' arms and legs, fished in her purse and handed them sticks of sugarless chewing gum, distributed kisses and hugs and walked back to the car with Dex.

"The sheriff, then?" he asked.

She considered, then shook her head no. "I don't think we'll bother the sheriff right yet," she said. "He only has a couple of deputies and one of them is off on maternity leave. Let's you and me poke around a little bit more, very carefully," here she fixed Dex with a Mom glare, "and see what we can learn."

Dex's face nearly split in two with his grin. "That's the stuff, Mrs. E.!"

But before that, Mrs. Entwhistle had to deal with her children.

~*~

Tommy and Diane had both called while she was out, and she'd been putting off returning their calls. It wasn't that she didn't want to talk to them; it was just that she knew what they were going to say, and she didn't want to hear it. Delaying the inevitable never worked, and that was demonstrated to her anew by the sight of Tommy's car in her driveway and both he and Diane waiting for her on the porch.

"Mama, where have you been?" Diane started before Mrs. Entwhistle could get herself up the steps.

"We've called and called and you didn't answer," she added in the same whiney voice she used when she was three.

"We got worried about you," Tommy said.

"I'm sorry, I planned to call you back today. I've just been real busy," Mrs. Entwhistle said meekly. "And you only left one message each."

"Whatever, Mama. You know we worry if we can't reach you."

Mrs. Entwhistle did not know that, but she thought it was sweet of them. "I appreciate your checking on me," she said. "Since I started working, I've been gone a lot."

"Yes, what about this job of yours?" Tommy asked. "We had to hear about it from other people. You're a reporter for the *Pantograph*? You're going to be seventy-nine on your next birthday. Do you think that's a suitable thing for you to be doing?"

Sometimes Tommy could sound like a grumpy little frog. Mrs. Entwhistle smiled at him fondly. "It's probably not, but I need the money."

"Need the money? Didn't Daddy leave you provided for?"

"He did, but his pension fund went bankrupt."

They took a minute to digest that.

"But what about all that money you won in the Publisher's Clearing House?" Tommy asked.

"I gave almost all of it away. And what's left, I promised to the grandkids. I don't intend to touch it."

Guilt rendered both Tommy and Diane speechless. They'd eagerly accepted new cars, cash, and college savings accounts for their kids out of those winnings. Their mother was ridiculously generous, and while they liked that trait when it was applied to themselves, they privately agreed she could have been more sensible when it came to other people.

Tommy cleared his throat. "I'd be happy to chip in if you need money."

"Me, too," Diane said in a small voice.

"And that's exactly why I didn't tell you about Dad's pension. You both have families of your own to tend to. I can take care of myself. There may come a day when I can't, and then I'll call on my children for help. But that day has not yet come." Mrs. Entwhistle spoke in her firmest voice, the same one that brooked no arguments when her children were little.

"But thank you for offering," she belatedly added. It was so hard sometimes, dealing with adult children. She wondered at what point they'd become the wise adults and she'd become the not-too-bright child who needed guidance and lectures.

"About the job, Mama," Diane said, "I understand you want to earn money, but isn't being a reporter hard work? Are you sure you're up to it? It's a slippery slope to an illness at your age."

Mrs. Entwhistle laughed. "I haven't slipped down that slope yet. It's good for me to get out and be involved in the community, don't you think? They say isolation is deadly for the elderly. Plus, I've got a remarkable young man working with me. His name is Dex, and you'd like him. He does all the hard stuff."

"I saw Jimmy Jack the other day," Tommy said, "and he told me about Dex. He said you're doing a great job, but he was worried you were doing too much, and that's why he wanted someone to help you."

Mrs. Entwhistle silently cursed Jimmy Jack. For someone who shrank from reporting the news, he sure was ready to blab about his employees. However, you catch more bees with honey, she reminded herself as she smiled into the worried faces of her children.

"Nonsense. Young people always think old people are doing too much. You forget we're made of tough stuff. After all, we raised you, didn't we? Now let's go inside, and I'll cut you each a piece of peach pie.

Maxine brought me some fresh peaches, and I baked yesterday. I believe I even have some vanilla ice cream to go on top."

That side-tracked them for the moment. If they'd known the full extent of her activities, the conversation would have been much longer. She sent up a silent plea that they'd never hear about the doggie-door escapade or the brick through the window.

Shell Game

Mr. Dansinger steepled his fingers in a gesture so like his father that Mrs. Entwhistle had to suppress a smile. He leaned back in his chair and looked at the ceiling for several long minutes.

"Here's what I've learned," he said. "Winterberry Wind Farms is a shell corporation registered in the Cayman Islands. The identity of the owners is masked with hired nominee directors. Winterberry Wind Farms has no products and no wind farm sites in the United States. There's no office and no employees. Yet as an entity, it can make financial transactions, open bank accounts, move funds and buy real estate. None of this is illegal. What is illegal is using a shell for hiding or laundering money, and evading taxes."

Dex and Mrs. Entwhistle nodded. They were soaking in the information, wondering how it applied to Booger's farm. A glimmer of comprehension shone on Mrs. Entwhistle's horizon.

Thinking aloud, she said, "So Winterberry Wind Farms might be holding a lot of money that it doesn't dare spend without authorities questioning its source. If it has a legitimate business, like a wind turbine farm on Booger's land, it could inflate the cost of the turbines and then inflate the profits and launder money that way. Right?"

"Right," Mr. Dansinger said. "There's no way of knowing what Winterberry Wind Farm's corporate assets are because it's an offshore shell. But if I was a betting man, I'd bet it's being used for money laundering."

"That would explain the level of violence when Booger tried to back out of their deal," Dex said. "You don't get beaten up as part of the negotiations in a normal business transaction."

"But why would such an operation come here, of all places?" Mrs. Entwhistle wondered. "I mean, we're just a dot on the map, not a big-time financial center."

"That may be the reason. Sometimes the least likely place is the safest," Mr. Dansinger said. "But there might be another reason. Winterberry Wind Farms has to have a registered agent to act on its behalf. That person is Giancarlo Cicerino. I don't know where the dirty money comes from, but the usual source is drugs. He may be in a very dangerous situation."

Mrs. Entwhistle had had her suspicions, but she was

dismayed to hear them confirmed. She actually had trouble drawing a breath for a minute. Dex patted her back in alarm, and Mr. Dansinger came around his desk to pour her a glass of water.

Why do people always think a glass of water will help? she wondered, but she sipped just to be polite.

"I'm flummoxed," she said, fanning her face with her hand. "Giancarlo has changed a lot since we were kids. I knew he'd gotten kind of sleazy. But I never would have thought he'd be part of anything really criminal."

"We don't know for sure that he is," Mr. Dansinger said cautiously. "It's all just conjecture at this point. I've done as much as I can do with the resources I have. It's too big for us; we need law enforcement."

"But not the sheriff," Mrs. Entwhistle murmured.

"No, indeed. Not the sheriff."

"Pete Peters," Mrs. Entwhistle said. "Just as soon as he gets home."

"Meanwhile, we'll gather all the evidence we can to save him time, right, Mrs. E.?" Dex asked, his face full of hope.

"What do you have in mind?"

"Do you think we could check with Booger again and see if he's gotten back any memory of the attack? We also need to let him know we found the agreement."

As far as they knew, Booger still thought the Winterberry Wind farm documents were in an envelope hidden among the ancient canned peaches. But he was home from the hospital now, and while he wouldn't be able to negotiate the cellar stairs for a while, he could send Caleb down to fetch them. Who knew what Booger would do if the papers weren't where he'd left them? Mrs. Entwhistle agreed that a visit was in order.

They stopped by the bakery, picked up a box of doughnut holes to sweeten the deal, and made their way to the farm. Caleb's truck was parked close to the house, and Booger was in his usual place on the front porch. He rocked steadily as he watched them approach.

"Good morning, Booger," Mrs. Entwhistle said as she climbed the steps. "It's good to see you home. You're looking well."

"I look like hell," he said shortly. "Who you got with you?"

"This is Dex Shofield. He came to see you when you were in the hospital, do you remember?"

"There's a lot about them days I don't remember a'tall. What's your business, Dex?"

"I'm just Mrs. Entwhistle's helper," Dex said with becoming humility. "Good to see you again, sir."

Booger visibly softened at being addressed as sir. Mrs. Entwhistle wondered whether he secretly coveted a more respectful form of address now that he was an old man. After all, he hadn't eaten boogers in a long time. Mrs. Entwhistle hoped.

"We've got something to tell you," she said, settling herself in a rocking chair. "And Caleb, too. Could we get him to join us?"

When they were all settled with the box of doughnut holes within easy reach, she told them what she and Dex had just learned about Winterberry Wind Farms.

"I hope I've explained it right," she finished. "It's so complicated, I don't understand it completely. But that's the gist of it: Winterberry Wind Farms is not a legitimate business."

"Well, I sorta figured that out when they whupped me upside the head," Booger said, and to everyone's surprise, he snorted with laughter.

"Wait a minute, sir," Dex said, "do you mean you've remembered who beat you?"

"It come back to me gradual when I was in the hospital, but I kept quiet about it. I didn't know the fellas that come here, but they was askin' for the contract, had I signed it, where was it and all. I told 'em I needed more time to think on it, but they said time was up, and they needed the papers right that minute, real bossy-like. Made me mad. I wouldn't 'a give it to 'em then if they'd been offerin' sacks of gold nuggets."

"Did you pull out your shotgun?" Mrs. Entwhistle asked.

"You betcha. But one of 'em just grabbed the barrel a'fore I could even raise it, and then the whupping started. I woke up a minute when they drug me out to the shed, but I couldn't stay awake. I reckon they looked around the place real good, but they didn't find what they was after." Booger nodded with satisfaction.

"We might have scared them away when we came to see you that day," Mrs. Entwhistle said. "There's more to tell you."

The story of her and Dex's midnight visit was related. She tried to pass over the part about the doggie door, but Booger stopped her.

"Now wait jest a minute," he said. "How'd you say you got into my house?"

"We didn't break in," she said evasively.

"No, but how, then?"

"Through the doggie door," she muttered.

"*You* went through that little bitty door?"

"Well, not all at once. It was kind of in two stages."

"You got stuck, didn't you?"

"I did, yes." Mrs. Entwhistle could feel her cheeks growing warm.

"That explains it!" Booger said, clapping his beefy palms together. "Caleb, get that piece of cloth."

Caleb returned waving a six-inch strip of Floyd's pants. "We couldn't figure out how this came to be stuck in the dog door," he said. He tried hard to keep a straight face, but finally he gave up.

Father and son laughed until their eyes streamed

with tears. "I'd give cash money to've seen that, Cora," Booger said. "Young man, was you a witness?"

"Uh, yes sir, I was there." Dex couldn't keep the grin off his face.

"Okay, let's just say it was funny and move on, shall we?" Mrs. Entwhistle said. "I've got more to say, if you gentleman are done laughing at my expense."

"Well, I reckon we're about done. I might laugh some more later, though, when I think about it again."

Mrs. Entwhistle resumed her narrative. When she got to the part about hiding in the cellar, Booger sat straight up in his chair and narrowed his eyes. She finished by taking the brown Winterberry Wind Farms envelope out of her purse and handing it over.

"Guess it wasn't hid as good as I thought," was Booger's only comment.

"Dad? What if they come back?" Caleb asked. "They still don't have what they wanted, and they wanted it bad enough to beat the crap out of you. We aren't safe here."

"I have an idea," Mrs. Entwhistle said. "There have been items in the 'Palaver' that suggest someone knows something about stealing in the Booster Club. That's run by Sissy Smith, and she's been appropriating funds for her own use. Her dad is Giancarlo Cicerino. He's an investor in Winterberry Wind Farms, and Sissy is pushing hard to get in on that investment. She thinks she can recoup what she's stolen from the Booster Club that way. So there's a connection between the Cicerinos, the Booster Club funds, and Winterberry Wind Farms. If we're right about Winterberry Wind Farms being a front for laundering money, that would account for the level of violence we've seen from those people. It's all connected, all this thievery and crime. What would you think about planting an item in the 'Palaver' to shake things up? We'd want to let the Winterberry people know the documents are no longer here at the farm, and also convey that someone is wise to them."

"But we aren't, totally," Dex said with an air of puzzlement.

"No, not yet, but we're getting there. What I'm thinking is something that won't make sense to most readers, but will speak to the people we want to reach."

"Do you think the Winterberry people, whoever they are, read the *Pantograph*?" Caleb asked.

"I know Giancarlo does, and that's all we need," Mrs. Entwhistle said. "Now how about these two items: One says, 'What you seek is safe in a bank vault,' and the other says, 'Who's boosting the Booster Club funds?' What do you think?"

"The one about the bank vault sounds pretty obscure," Dex said, scratching his head. "Do you think the people you want to reach will get it?"

"The only person who has to get it is Giancarlo, and I think he'll understand exactly what we're saying. He can explain it to his bosses."

"So, you don't think he's the brains of the operation?"

"Who, Giancarlo? Gracious, no!" Mrs. Entwhistle laughed. "Somebody's pulling his strings, for sure, and we need to know who."

Sissy Spills The Beans

Mrs. Entwhistle hadn't seen Maxine for a week. When she realized that, she walked directly to the front hall where the landline phone lived and called her.

"Max, are we still friends?" she said when Maxine picked up. "I'm so sorry I've been neglecting you."

"No, now Cora, no, you haven't. You've just been busy." Maxine was never one to harbor hurt feelings.

"If I'm too busy for my best friend, I'm too busy," Mrs. Entwhistle said. "Are you free to come for lunch?"

"I have the doctor at ten, but I can come after that. Thank you, Cora, I'd love to."

Mrs. Entwhistle went to some trouble. She made a cheese and mushroom quiche, picked some ripe tomatoes and baby lettuce from her garden for a salad, and baked her special yeast rolls. For dessert, she put together a blackberry cobbler, Maxine's favorite. She set the table with cloth placemats and napkins and gathered some garden flowers for a centerpiece. She had some making up to do.

Maxine ate appreciatively, even accepting a second helping of quiche. "My, that was good," she said, giving her lips one more swipe with her napkin. "You must have cooked all morning. I hate for you to take so much trouble just for me, though. We could have gone to McDonald's."

Maxine had a secret passion for French fries which she seldom indulged, but she was always on the lookout for an excuse.

"With all those screaming young'uns running around, and their mamas glued to their phones and not paying the least bit of attention? We can't talk privately at McDonald's, and I've got things to tell you." Mrs. Entwhistle launched into her story of wind farms, money laundering, home invasions, close calls, and Booster Club malfeasance.

Maxine heard her out in silence, her eyes getting bigger and bigger. When Mrs. Entwhistle finally ran out of steam and stopped to wet her whistle with a sip of iced tea, Maxine said, "Why, my stars! No wonder you haven't called me. Money laundering in our little town, and Giancarlo right in the middle of it. That old fool will get himself killed if he doesn't watch out. And how does he think it helps Sissy to involve her in an illegal scheme?"

"I'm not sure either of them have thought it all the

way through," Mrs. Entwhistle said. "Sissy is in a panic, apparently, and that's not conducive to logic. And here's a part I didn't tell you: Giancarlo is sick. He said he has cancer and doesn't have long to live."

"Oh, the poor man. Remember, I said I thought he didn't look well. Does Sissy know?"

"I doubt it. But she needs to, doesn't she? I don't believe in keeping secrets like that in a family. People need to be able to say their last goodbyes and make things right if they need to. Once a loved one dies, it's too late for anything but regrets."

They were silent for a moment, thinking of the finality of that last breath.

"Are you going to tell her?"

"I'll have to think about it."

Mrs. Entwhistle didn't relish the task. It was never pleasant to be the bearer of bad news, and she really preferred to keep out of other people's business as much as possible. Not that she'd been doing that lately, she thought guiltily. She was in Booger's business about as far as she could get.

"Being a reporter is harder than I thought it would be," she confessed to Maxine. "Just writing up meetings and such, that's easy. But all this other stuff, I don't know how I got so wound up in it."

"That's just the way you are," Max said. "You're always whole-hearted in whatever you're doing. You're just not one to do things half-way. Remember the Meals on Wheels people?"

Mrs. Entwhistle smiled. "I went to Angela and J.C.'s wedding. I wonder how J.C. likes living with all those cats."

Roger looked up anxiously. He'd caught the word "cats" and was troubled there might be one lurking about. His recent run-in with the big orange tomcat from next door had not been one of his finer moments. In fact, he'd run yipping to Mrs. Entwhistle with four bloody scratches on his tender black nose.

"Never mind, Rog," Mrs. Entwhistle said now, smoothing his ears. "Go back to sleep."

With a sigh, the little dog put his head on his paws and closed his eyes again. The ladies regarded him tenderly. Roger wouldn't be with them much longer. Old dogs and old friends were precious, and that made the news of Giancarlo's illness hard to bear. He was a rascal, a shady and disreputable character, but they'd played together as children, and they remembered his high school glory days. It was hard to think of a world that didn't contain him somewhere, even if years went by when they didn't see him.

"Well." Mrs. Entwhistle said with finality. "Enough sad talk."

She rose and began stacking the dishes. Maxine helped, and they left the kitchen as clean as if no meal had ever been prepared there.

"What would you like to do this afternoon?"

"Would you mind if we went to the mall?" Maxine

asked. "I've got a coupon for Macy's that expires tomorrow, and I want to look at sheets."

"Sure, we can go to the mall. I've got a list somewhere." Mrs. Entwhistle dug through her purse and finally produced a dog-eared piece of paper with a few items scrawled on it. They were things she couldn't get anywhere except the shopping mall. She hated to go, and put it off as long as possible, but it wouldn't be too bad to go with Maxine.

Maxine drove, since her car was already in the driveway. The big Lincoln Navigator was a challenge for a short person like Maxine, but she'd learned to handle it. She swung it into a parking space so small that Mrs. Entwhistle closed her eyes and clamped her mouth shut to keep from crying out a warning. Canned music wafted them through the revolving door to the mall, and Mrs. Entwhistle took out her list.

It was a sorrow to Maxine that when they shopped together, she never had time to browse. It was all business; get in, check off purchases, get out. But she knew her friend detested shopping, so she didn't complain. If she really needed to browse, she came alone.

As they walked along briskly, Mrs. Entwhistle suddenly stopped and grabbed Maxine's arm. "Lookie there," she whispered, jerking her head toward a store window. Maxine peered through the plate glass.

"Why, I believe that's Sissy Smith," she said, "Yoo-hoo, Sissy, hello!"

That wasn't quite what Mrs. Entwhistle had in mind; she'd hoped to observe Sissy, watch covertly and see what she was up to. Too late for that now. They joined Sissy at the register, where she was paying for a large rolling suitcase.

"Oh, hello," Sissy said unenthusiastically. Mrs. Entwhistle remembered they hadn't parted on the best of terms last time they'd spoken.

"Taking a trip?" Maxine asked.

"I'm getting this for Butch, for his...birthday. It's next week," Sissy said.

Mrs. Entwhistle distinctly remembered that Butch's birthday was in the winter, because his and Tommy's birthdays were close together, and they'd often joined forces for a little party. She didn't say anything. Let's see where Sissy is going with this, she thought.

"Yes, Butch has always wanted a large suitcase on wheels," Sissy went on, "and I just thought I'd surprise him with one on his birthday. He likes to travel, but he always over packs. Men! I think they take more clothes than women do simply because they're too lazy to plan, so they just throw in everything."

Sissy's laugh didn't sound like she was amused. Mrs. Entwhistle observed with interest that she was giving too much information. Liars did that. Thought it made them more believable.

"I wouldn't have figured Butch for a flowery print like that. Will you be going with him on this trip?"

she asked.

"Oh, we don't have anything planned just at the moment," Sissy said, glancing wildly around the store as if hoping for rescue. "I'm just, uh, just thinking ahead."

"That's always a good idea," Maxine said. She sensed that the conversation had undercurrents, but she had no idea what they were.

"Maybe you'd like to discuss your trip with me sometime," Mrs. Entwhistle said. "I find it helps to talk over plans with a third party who has no ax to grind."

"Ax to grind?" Maxine looked confused.

"Yeah, no, that's okay," Sissy said. "It's probably too late to talk about it. Things – plans – have gone too far."

"It's not too late," Mrs. Entwhistle said firmly. "It's never too late to do the right thing."

"But people could get hurt," Sissy said, and her eyes filled with tears. "Have gotten hurt."

"All the more reason to go very carefully," Mrs. Entwhistle said.

"Hurt? Are you going somewhere dangerous?" Maxine asked, trying her best to get a handle on this very puzzling conversation.

"Maybe you'd like to pay me a visit," Mrs. Entwhistle said.

"I've really got to run," Sissy said, grabbing the big

suitcase and yanking it behind her as she headed for the door. She cast one glance back at Mrs. Entwhistle before she disappeared.

Maxine looked after her and then at Mrs. Entwhistle. "What was that all about?" she asked.

"I'll tell you in the car. Come on, let's go."

"But I haven't looked at sheets." Maxine protested. "I've got this coupon."

"Sorry, sorry, but I have to get home. I have a feeling I'm about to have company."

It was dark before she heard a knock on her door. She opened it to Sissy, who stood indecisively on the threshold, blinking in the light from the hall.

"Let's sit out here on the porch," Mrs. Entwhistle suggested. She knew confessions were made more easily under cover of darkness.

They settled on the swing. Sissy was shivering. Mrs. Entwhistle tucked a quilt over her legs and patted her knee. "Now, tell me what's going on."

That was all Sissy needed. She was obviously dying to unburden her guilty conscience, and the words came out in a rush.

"See, Butch and I, our marriage isn't what you think. It's... We've grown apart. He's more like my brother than my husband, and now that the kids are grown, we have nothing to talk about anymore. He's a good person, we're just not very interested in each other anymore. I think it would be better if we cut our losses and called it quits."

"How long have you been married?" Mrs. Entwhistle asked.

"Almost thirty years."

"That's a lot of years to toss in the trash heap."

"I know. But isn't it better to live what life we have left in happiness rather than this... trap... that we're in now?"

"Well, let's think about that. You and Butch are bored with each other, is that right?"

"Yes. It sounds silly when you say it like that, but yes, that's about it. We have nothing in common."

"Except adult children, grandchildren soon, thirty years of working and living together, your home, your community."

"But there's no excitement! It's just all so blah. That's why I started--" Sissy broke off.

"Started embezzling from the Booster Club?"

Sissy hung her head. "Yes," she whispered. "How did you know?"

"Look, it's going to come out. Something like this always does. You can't run away from it."

"Yes, I can! My Dad will help me. There's a business deal he's working on, and he's trying to get me in on it, too. When it's finalized we'll have plenty of cash. I'll pay back the Booster Club and go home with Dad. He'll help me make a fresh start in California."

"It would be a tragic mistake to count on your father for that."

"Why? What do you mean?"

"He hasn't told you, has he?"

~*~

Sissy cried for a long time after Mrs. Entwhistle told her about Giancarlo's diagnosis. In fact, she cried so alarmingly that Mrs. Entwhistle wondered if she'd done the right thing. Maybe it was just everything together, though. Her father's illness on top of her own criminal activity, and her marriage on the rocks. Well, that would be plenty to cry about, wouldn't it?

When Sissy finally dried up, Mrs. Entwhistle made tea and toast. She felt like comfort food was needed. "Won't Butch be worried about where you are this late?" she asked Sissy.

"I don't care if he is."

"Well, I care. Either go home, or call and tell him you're here with me."

"He's probably asleep by now. He's used to me staying out late. He just goes to bed. He doesn't care."

"Like I said: go home or call him. You won't worry your husband in my house."

Sissy shrugged and reached for her phone, but paused. "Do you think... I mean, could I stay here tonight? I'll just sleep on the sofa, I won't be any trouble. I feel too tired to move."

Mrs. Entwhistle really wanted some peace and quiet. A hot bath, a quiet house, her own bed. But looking at Sissy, she knew the poor soul needed care. It didn't matter that she was a thief and a liar; she was a person.

"Of course, you can," Mrs. Entwhistle said. "Right after you call Butch."

Sissy dialed and Mrs. Entwhistle could hear from her side of the conversation that Butch had not been asleep and had indeed been worrying. He seemed to have trouble understanding why Sissy was staying over at Mrs. Entwhistle's. Finally, Sissy said, "Because I want to, that's why," and hung up her phone.

Immediately, she curled up on her side on the sofa and fell asleep like she'd been knocked on the head. Mrs. Entwhistle spread the Afghan over her, turned out the lights and went to bed.

Pete Peters Comes Home

"From what you're telling me, they haven't really done anything wrong yet," Pete Peters said. Rumpled and unshaven from his early morning flight from the West Coast, he sat across the kitchen table from Mrs. Entwhistle and Dex.

"They beat up Booger. I'd say that was wrong," Mrs. Entwhistle said indignantly.

"Sure, that was assault, and it's a crime. I meant the money laundering part. A wind farm is certainly not a typical vehicle for that. Usually, criminals go in for high cash flow, high turnover businesses like casinos. Although," Pete paused thoughtfully, "maybe they think that since a wind farm would be an unlikely place, it would be the last place law enforcement would look. That may be the attraction. In any case, the turbine deal is still in the planning stage. The crooks may be sitting on a pile of dirty money, but until they get their hands on the signed contract, they can't go forward."

"The contract's in the vault at the bank, and we planted an item in the 'Palaver' to let Giancarlo know that so he can pass the information along to his cohorts. I don't want them coming after poor old Booger again."

Caleb was staying with his dad, and both men kept their firearms handy. It was doubtful that the most determined bad guy would get to Booger now, but still Mrs. Entwhistle worried.

"I'll contact the proper authorities at the FBI, and Mr. Dansinger, as a banker, will file a Suspicious Activity Report with the Financial Crimes Enforcement Network at the Department of Treasury. They'll take it from there," Pete said. "I wouldn't be surprised if they are already watching these guys."

"What about Giancarlo? He's mixed up in it somehow, but I don't know the extent of his involvement. He's a sick old man, Pete, not long for this world. It would be a shame to end his life in disgrace."

"All I can do is pass on the facts of the case; then it's out of my hands. Depending on what they find, they may settle for breaking up the syndicate behind Winterberry Wind Farms and killing this one deal, at least. Of course, the crooks will try again someplace else, but you can't arrest folks for what they might do in the future. More's the pity."

"What about Sissy and the Booster Club?" Dex asked.

"Different kettle of fish," Pete replied. "That's a local matter and should be dealt with by the local authorities. Has anyone reported it to the sheriff?"

"We haven't," Mrs. Entwhistle said. "Sissy thinks she can get out of this mess without anyone being the wiser."

"That may be impossible."

After Pete left, with a promise to keep them informed, Mrs. Entwhistle noticed Dex seemed unusually quiet. His mischievous brown eyes lacked their usual sparkle; in fact, he looked downright pensive.

"What's the matter?" she asked him.

"Oh, nothing, really. It's just sad. Sad when people screw up their lives so needlessly," Dex replied. "I mean, Sissy and Butch are, like, pillars of the community, they've been married forever, beautiful home, raised kids, and now they could be enjoying life. But are they? No, they're screwing it up with stealing and throwing rocks through windows."

"Yes, people do manage to get themselves in some peculiar situations. Those are some pretty deep thoughts for someone your age," Mrs. Entwhistle said. "What brought that on?"

"I guess I was thinking of my folks and how happy they'd be just to have a chance at normal lives," Dex said.

He'd never spoken about his family, other than to

say he had a brother two years older. Mrs. Entwhistle didn't know anything else about Dex except what she saw -- a bright, engaging twenty-one year-old with a foot in each camp of boyhood and manhood. He had nice manners and was obviously well educated. She knew he was brave and adventurous and funny. Altogether, a young man after her heart. Now her curiosity was aroused.

"Tell me about your family," she said, and leaned forward to listen.

"Mom's a stay-at-home-mom and Dad is a civil engineer. They make a good pair, because she's intuitive and he's methodical. I guess they never expected anything except an ordinary life, but then Alex was born."

"Your brother. What happened?"

"Alex was in trouble from day one, they told me. He didn't get enough oxygen or something; anyway, he has brain damage. Developmentally, he's about four, although he's actually two years older than I."

Mrs. Entwhistle nodded. "That must be tough for your parents."

"They're really strong, but yeah, it's tough. Alex's needs have to come first. His doctor and therapy appointments, his special school, it all takes a lot of time and money and attention. And then he can be really hard to live with. Tantrums, running away, sleep problems. He can't help it, but that doesn't make it any easier. Mom and Dad are worn out now that they're older, and Alex is a full-grown man and hard to handle. He probably needs to be placed in some kind of care, but they say they'll never do that. I know they worry about what will become of him after they die. I told them I'd always make sure Alex is taken care of, but they try to plan and save for his future."

"So what did your family situation lead you to decide about yourself?" she asked.

He looked up, surprised. "How did you know I decided anything?"

"You did, though, didn't you?"

"Yes, actually, I did. I decided when I was about twelve not to cause my parents any trouble. I'd get good grades, go to college, and land a good job. Just be the kid who didn't need a lot of attention."

"I'm sure your folks appreciate it."

"I guess they do, in a distracted kind of way. Alex takes up most of their resources and thoughts. They were glad not to have to worry about me, and when I brought home good report cards or won an award or something in school they'd try to rally some enthusiasm, but they were exhausted. It's okay, though, I don't need to be praised."

Oh, yes, you do; we all do, Mrs. Entwhistle thought, but she only nodded. "How did you get interested in journalism?"

"I volunteered on the high school paper, and the faculty advisor was great. It never seemed like work to me, it was just fun. When it came time to pick my college major, I remembered Dad saying, 'Do what you love and you'll never work a day in your life.'"

"Do your parents approve of your career choice?"

"I think they wish I'd chosen something that paid better, but they're happy I've found my niche. Alex had to go into the hospital for a lung infection the same weekend I told them, so we never got a chance to talk it all the way through."

"I'm sorry your family has had such trials," Mrs. Entwhistle said. "In a way, it's taken away a lot from your life. But what I see is a young man who uses adversity as a way to grow strong. You've got a bright mind, a willingness to work hard, and a drive to succeed. And best of all, you don't need cheerleaders to urge you on; you're motivated all by yourself. You're going to be a great success, Dex Shofield, you mark my words now."

Dex actually blushed. Then he stood, leaned down and kissed Mrs. Entwhistle's cheek.

Pete called the next day. "I talked to the FBI, and they're starting an investigation," he said. "They'll do some surveillance, check Mr. Cicerino's background, pull up similar cases to see if some of the same people are involved. It might take them a while; they don't move at lightning speed, but be patient. The wheels are turning now."

"Thank you, Pete, you always know just what to do," Mrs. Entwhistle said warmly.

"Not always. Remember that time you were mixed up in the Witness Protection Program and I didn't know what to do with you?"

"How could I ever forget? Do you still have that bullet lodged in your leg?"

"Sure do. It predicts rain better than any weather forecaster."

They could laugh about it now, but it wasn't funny at the time. Pete had nearly lost his life, and he liked to say that Mrs. Entwhistle had saved him. She remembered very little of the shoot-out, having hit her head a good lick just as it happened, but she was glad if she'd had some little part in saving Pete. He was one of her favorite people, he and now Dex. She paused for a moment to wonder why she had such rapport with young people other than her own. She loved her son, Tommy, but he was a perpetual mystery to her, and her daughter, Diane, was a puzzle wrapped in an enigma. Ah well, families! She'd hoped it would all become clear to her in old age, but as her seventy-ninth birthday rose on the horizon, she had to admit it wasn't likely.

Sissy Gets Away With It

"So, I told him, 'Butch, I said, there's something I have to talk to you about,'" Sissy said, looking earnestly at Mrs. Entwhistle. She'd taken to confiding in her since the night she spent on Mrs. Entwhistle's sofa.

"And Butch said, 'let's sit down and you tell me all about it,' so I did. And it was so embarrassing when he kept asking me why I did it, why I'd steal from the Booster Club, and didn't I know I could have anything I wanted, that it was our money, not his money. Then I had to tell him I needed money because I wanted to leave him."

Sissy paused and looked dramatically distressed. "You know, he actually cried. Big tough Butch, he cried when I said that."

Mrs. Entwhistle thought Sissy was enjoying it too much. "That should be private between the two of you," she said repressively, "I don't need to hear your personal business."

Sissy nodded, chastened, but she couldn't restrain her narrative drive. "So then I said, 'Butch, please don't cry.' And he said, 'Sissy, I just can't lose you, I love you more than life itself.' That really touched me, when he said life itself. I didn't think Butch cared, you see."

Sissy said she and Butch had talked long into the night, having the most open and thoughtful conversation in all their years of marriage. He'd confessed that he suspected her of stealing from Booster Club funds, but he didn't know why she was doing it and was afraid to ask her. All he could think about was how to keep people from finding out. Panicked when he realized Mrs. Entwhistle was pursuing the story, he'd thrown the brick through her window to scare her off.

"He's very, very sorry about that," Sissy said. "He wasn't thinking clearly."

She had to tell Butch that she was bored and wanted more excitement in her life. Here, Sissy giggled. "He said he was just the man to bring it!"

Mrs. Entwhistle interrupted hastily at that point. "Okay, okay, let's just say you and Butch made up. Don't put any visuals in my head, I have to see you both around town."

Sissy giggled again.

"What are you going to do about the Booster Club?" Mrs. Entwhistle asked.

"I still have some of the money because I was saving it to run away. Butch is making up the rest. I'll just put it back in the Booster Club account. I was really only kind of borrowing it, wasn't I? I would have paid it back."

"You'd have paid it back if you'd been able to invest in the wind turbines, right?"

"Right. It might still work out, but if it does, Butch and I will use the money to travel or something."

"And that's it? Nobody ever knows, you just cover up what you did and go on?"

"Well... Yes. Why not? What good would it do to tell people? My family would be ashamed, and it would cause hard feelings all around."

"There are such things as consequences, Sissy Smith. When you do wrong, you should accept responsibility. What you're doing is more sneaking around and letting Butch bail you out. You were ready to ditch him, so ready that you stole money to finance your getaway, but now you're accepting his help to cover it all up and let you off scot-free."

"He *is* my husband," Sissy said stiffly. "It's only natural that he'd want to help me."

"He's your *enabler*," Mrs. Entwhistle said. She felt as angry at Sissy as she could remember feeling at anybody, even though at one time she'd felt sorry for her. To control her temper, she went into the backyard where she paced the length of her zinnia bed. Goldfinches and butterflies hovered over the flowers, the sun shone like a blessing, and Mrs.

Entwhistle felt her anger slip away.

None of my business. What the Smiths do is absolutely none of my business. I'm not the judge and jury, I'm not the fixer, and I can't do a thing about their decisions.

After a while, she felt calm again and went back inside to where Sissy still sat at the kitchen table. Mrs. Entwhistle was gratified to see that she looked ashamed as she sat back down with her.

"So your troubles seem to be solved," she said, "except for your father."

Tears immediately sprang into Sissy's eyes. "Oh, poor Daddy! I'll never get over how he came to help me when he was so sick, and I was too wrapped up in myself to even notice. If you hadn't told me, I don't know if I'd have figured it out yet."

"Have you talked to him in the last couple of days?"

"No, but I'm having lunch with him today. Do you want join us?"

"I think you and your father need time together alone," Mrs. Entwhistle said. "Give him my best."

Later, Sissy told her she went to the Busy Bee Diner and sat at a table waiting for more than two hours. Giancarlo never showed up and didn't answer his cell phone. Finally, not sure whether to be worried or angry, Sissy went looking for him. She drove to his motel room and, when she got no response to her knock, asked the front desk to unlock the door. Inside, the room looked like it had been hit with a strong wind. The bed linens were on the floor, the mattress was askew on the frame, drawers were pulled out and tossed around, the only chair was upside down, and all Giancarlo's expensive clothes, of which he took immaculate care, were strewn about the room. His wallet, cell phone, and sunglasses were still on the bedside table.

Sissy had the sense to call Butch. Butch had the sense to call Mrs. Entwhistle, who drove right over and surveyed the chaos while the two of them filled her in.

"Who would do this?" Sissy demanded through tears. "Has someone taken Daddy? Why would they do that?"

All Butch could seem to do was pat Sissy consolingly on the back and say there, there. Mrs. Entwhistle took charge.

"Butch, make sure Giancarlo's room is paid up. Tell the desk clerk – it's Joe Phipps – that your father-in-law is coming to stay with you and Sissy for a few days, but he wants to keep his room. Ask that the maid stay out, say Giancarlo wants everything just the way he left it. We need to keep the room intact in case it's (here she lowered her voice) a crime scene."

Butch hurried off, glad to have someone tell him what to do.

"Sissy, tears aren't going to help find your dad. I have a feeling I know who's behind this and what they were looking for. We have to figure out how to get in touch with them so we can negotiate

Giancarlo's return."

That turned out not to be hard. Sissy's cell rang a few minutes later, and she listened with ever-widening eyes. She pressed Speaker so Mrs. Entwhistle could hear, too.

"We've got your dad," a raspy, unfamiliar male voice said, "and if you want to see him alive again, you'll do what we say."

"Wh-what do you want?" Sissy asked.

"We want the signed contract."

"I don't know what you're talking about. I don't have any contract."

"Ask that old hag standing next to you, she knows all about it."

Both women shot anxious glances at the window. Mrs. Entwhistle was prepared to overlook the "old hag" designation, but she did object to being spied on. Sissy's phone went dark. The caller hung up.

~*~

Pete, Dex, Mrs. Entwhistle and Butch sat in a semi-circle around Mr. Dansinger's desk in the bank. This was a council of war.

Pete spoke first. "Let's sum up: the people who took Giancarlo are demanding the signed Winterberry Wind Farm contract as ransom. That contract is in this bank's vault right now, just a few feet from where we're sitting. The landowner changed his mind about going through with it, but that got him a beating. What concerns me most is the violence that's being used to try to ram this deal through. Surely there are many other sites for a wind farm if your main objective is to create a means of laundering money."

"We don't know who's behind it," Mrs. Entwhistle said. "Maybe whoever it is just isn't too smart, or very good at being a criminal. Maybe they don't know when to cut their losses and move on."

"Possibly," Pete said. "Criminals are not masterminds, in my experience. Right now, we have to figure out how to get the contract to these guys, whoever they are, and get Giancarlo back."

"We're just going to hand it over?" Dex asked incredulously.

"Sure. It's a worthless piece of paper. How could it be enforced? To a judge, it would actually be evidence of a plan to commit a crime. So, sure, we'll hand it over," Pete said, "after we photocopy it."

Mr. Dansinger rose from his desk, went to the teller line and motioned to the head teller to join him. They walked to the vault's steel door, turned their backs on each other and simultaneously twirled the two combination locks that guarded the vault.

"Neither of them can open the vault alone," Dex whispered. It seemed like such a solemn occasion that whispering was appropriate. "They have to open their locks at the same time, and neither knows both combinations." He shrugged. "I saw a movie about it."

Mr. Dansinger returned holding the Winterberry Wind Farms contract. "Here it is," he said unnecessarily. "Who's going to take charge of it?"

"Me, for now," Pete said. "When we hear from the kidnappers again, we'll figure out how to handle the drop."

"I'll meet them," Dex said. "When they call, tell them I'll exchange the contract for Giancarlo."

Pete Peters nodded. He couldn't do it himself, since he was well-known in the community as a federal lawman. Dex would be a strong and agile substitute. It seemed like a good plan. To them.

The kidnappers had different ideas. When the phone call came a few hours later, the raspy voice said, "Send the old lady."

"Mrs. Entwhistle? No way," Pete protested.

"Then where do you want us to leave Giancarlo's body?"

"I'll do it," Mrs. Entwhistle said clearly. The phone was on speaker; she knew she could be heard. "When and where?"

Neighbors Can Be Too Good

"You certainly have to give them points for originality," Mrs. Entwhistle said. "Who'd ever think they'd choose the Busy Bee Diner? I'm beginning to think they really are stupid."

"Or maybe it's a brilliant plan," Dex said. "The other customers could actually be used as hostages if the kidnappers get cornered. They could grab someone as a human shield."

"Sometimes the way your mind works scares me a little," Mrs. Entwhistle said, eyeing Dex warily. "You get all this criminal knowledge from movies?"

"That and reading," Dex admitted, grinning.

Pete was finally having that talk with the sheriff they'd all been postponing. He said they couldn't very well carry out a ransom demand in broad daylight on Main Street without involving local law enforcement. Mrs. Entwhistle fervently hoped

Sheriff Trevino was sharper than she thought he was.

Pete's hand preceded him through the door, thumb sticking up. "He's with us," Pete said. "Not a bad guy at all. It took me a while to explain everything to him. It's a complicated story, and I had to be very tactful about why we left him in the dark until now. Didn't want to start out with him being all defensive and angry."

"So will he go along with our plan?" Mrs. Entwhistle asked.

"Not only will he go along with it, he made some good suggestions," Pete said. "He's not happy about you being the go-between, Mrs. Entwhistle, but he agreed that we have to comply with the kidnappers' demands. He's getting three deputies from out of town and deploying them in the diner. He'll make sure they're from far enough out of town so no one recognizes them. He and I will be outside, out of sight, but where we can see and hear everything."

"Where?" Dex asked.

"It'll be better if you don't know. You might glance our way inadvertently. We don't want the kidnappers to follow your gaze right to us."

"I wouldn't be that obvious."

"I'm sure you wouldn't. Still, it's much easier if you really don't know where we are. Just trust us, we'll be there."

~*~

The exchange was to take place the next morning at eleven. Mrs. Entwhistle surmised that the kidnappers had chosen that time because breakfast would be over and lunch not yet begun. There'd be a few people in the diner, but not many. She'd take a seat by the window and place the Winterberry Wind Farms contract in its brown envelope on the table in plain sight. When a black Ford Explorer pulled up at the curb, she was to get up and leave. The kidnapper would come in, sit at her table, pick up the envelope and then follow her out. Giancarlo would be in the Explorer. When the kidnaper emerged from the diner carrying the contract, Giancarlo would be put out on the sidewalk. It sounded simple.

Pete and Sheriff Trevino would be waiting nearby, and at the moment Giancarlo set foot out of the car, one of them would grab him and hustle him to safety. Mrs. Entwhistle wasn't clear about what came after that. She guessed there was a plan to apprehend the car and the people in it. She hoped so.

Meanwhile, she dressed carefully for her part. Her second-best black pants, sneakers (which looked awful with those pants, but she had to be able to move fast if necessary), a white shirt so she'd be easily visible, and her big shoulder-bag to hold the envelope. At the last minute, she added her straw hat.

She was in place at ten-fifty five. Her progress to her table was slowed by the need to say hello to all the folks she knew. She ignored the three out-of-town deputies, who looked like cops even in plain clothes.

She hoped the kidnapper wouldn't think so, too. Finally she took her seat by the window and Carol Ann brought her a steaming cup of tea without being asked.

Reaching in her shoulder bag, she pulled out the manila envelope and placed it conspicuously on the table. Then she placed her bag and hat on the empty chair. Try as she might, she couldn't keep her eyes from the window. Eleven o'clock came. And went. The minutes trudged by on little leaden feet. Mrs. Entwhistle felt a trickle of sweat run down her side. Were they not coming? She felt faint from nerves.

When she was about to give up hope, she saw a big black car idling slowly along the curb. It stopped. The windows were tinted so darkly it was impossible to discern the occupants. She watched as the passenger door opened and a man she'd never seen before got out. This was her cue. Rising, she grabbed her purse, plunked some bills on the table and started for the door just as it opened and the strange man entered.

"Oh, Mrs. Entwhistle, wait a minute, I'll get your check," Carol Anne called from behind the counter.

"Never mind, just keep the change," Mrs. Entwhistle said, with what she hoped was a jaunty wave.

"No, now, I need to ring it up or the cash won't come out right tonight. I'm sure you're due some change. And look, you left your hat. And your envelope! Why, Mrs. Entwhistle, I've never known you to be so forgetful. Are you all right, honey? You're white as a ghost. Do you not feel well? Shall I call someone?

Roberto, come here! Mrs. Entwhistle isn't feeling well."

Every head in the diner had turned by this time. No matter how vehement her protestations of perfect health were, a little crowd gathered including Roberto in his splotchy white cook's apron. She was seated and watered (*that darn glass of water again!*) and her belongings, including the brown envelope, were restored to her. Her wrists were rubbed and her back patted. When she finally convinced her kind neighbors that she was okay, the strange man was gone, the car was gone, and Giancarlo was gone. The deputies were standing on the sidewalk, and it looked like they were cursing.

Mrs. Entwhistle walked home with her head down. She'd had one job to do, the easiest one of all, and she'd blown it. How would they ever get Giancarlo back after this debacle? He was sick and needed her help, and she'd failed him. She'd failed everyone. Most of all, herself.

She barely looked up when Dex's long legs fell into step beside her. He remained mercifully quiet, just kept pace with her. After a while, he offered his arm. It did help to lean on him just a little bit at one of the most discouraging moments of her life. When they got to her porch, Pete and Sheriff Trevino were waiting. She couldn't bear to look at them.

"Mrs. Entwhistle, don't you feel bad about this," Pete said firmly. "You did exactly what you were supposed to do, it just went south. That happens sometimes – a lot of times – in undercover operations. They'll be back in touch. They don't have what they want, and they still have their bargaining chip in Giancarlo."

"I don't think I can go through it again," Mrs. Entwhistle confessed. "I feel all swimmy-headed. Maybe I am too old for this kind of work."

The men exchanged uneasy glances. They agreed, but each of them knew better than to say so.

"Hold on," Dex said, "I've got an idea."

~*~

Just as Pete said, the call came later that evening. Mrs. Entwhistle and the three men in her living room jumped when the phone rang. She punched the speaker button so they could all hear.

"Help me," said a wavering voice, "help me." It was Giancarlo, but he sounded ancient. And scared.

"You want us to kill this old man?" It was the same man from before; Mrs. Entwhistle felt she'd know his raspy snarl anywhere. "Take the contract to the park tonight at midnight and leave it on the bench beside the statue of Robert E. Lee. Just leave it and go. After we get it, we'll put Giancarlo out on the street somewhere, but you'll have to look for him because we ain't making it so easy for you this time. This is your last chance, or you'll be looking for a dead man. Don't fool around this time."

Mrs. Entwhistle had her mouth open to say, "No, please don't hurt him, he's sick," but before the words came out, the line went dead.

Dex nodded at Pete, and went up the stairs. When he came back down, he was wearing the black slacks, white blouse and straw hat she'd worn that morning. He couldn't get his feet into her sneakers, but his own would do.

"Good thing we're both tall and skinny," he said with a wink.

He was surprisingly believable dressed as her. The pant legs were too short and the shirt was tight across the shoulders, but with the hat on, in dim light and from a distance, he'd do.

"Remember to shorten your stride," Pete said, "you don't want to go loping along. Take little steps, like an old, I mean, mature lady. And carry your head forward a bit."

Mrs. Entwhistle bristled at that; she prided herself on her good posture. But she didn't say anything. It was no time for vanity. She was just thankful she wasn't the one walking through the park with that darned envelope. For once, she'd be more than happy to wait in the car.

"You can just stay right here at home," Sheriff Trevino said, patting her hand. "We'll take it from here."

"But I've been working on this from the beginning. I want to be in at the end," she protested.

"I don't think it's safe," the sheriff began, but Pete interrupted him.

"No, Mrs. Entwhistle's right. She and Dex broke this

case, and they've been ahead of us all the way. She deserves a chance to see it through."

Dex in Drag

Dex drove Mrs. Entwhistle's car to the park and situated it nose out in a parking space, just in case he had to leave in a hurry. Mrs. Entwhistle wasn't sure if her old car was capable of hurrying, but it would probably be faster than Dex's usual means of transportation, his little scooter.

She sat in the back seat of Pete's sedan watching as Dex walked with tiny (old lady!) steps, head thrust forward, hat hiding his face. I hope I don't walk like that, Mrs. Entwhistle thought. He approached the statue of Robert E. Lee, sat down on the bench at its base, removed the now-dog-eared brown envelope from Mrs. Entwhistle's tote bag and placed it beside him. He got to his feet with what he probably thought was an old lady struggle, minced back to the car and stood beside it. Nothing happened; no one appeared. He waited.

"Come on, Dex, get out of there," Pete muttered. "If

you really were Mrs. Entwhistle, you wouldn't be hanging around."

Dex obediently started the car and drove away. Mrs. Entwhistle knew he was mad at himself for not thinking beyond the drop. Now he had to head away from the action with no reason to return. But she'd underestimated Dex. Fifteen minutes later, the back door of Pete's car opened, making her jump in alarm. But it was just Dex, now in his own clothes, with a wicked gleam in his eyes.

"I took your car home, changed and got back here by way of a lot of shrubs and bushes," he explained. "Didn't think I was going to miss the grand finale, did you?"

"I might have known," Mrs. Entwhistle murmured.

"Are you sure you weren't seen?" Pete asked.

"Positive. I had my route planned, and I was super-careful. Didn't see a soul. I did run into the deputy stationed on this side of the park, but he recognized me and let me pass."

They sat and watched and waited. Mrs. Entwhistle stifled several large yawns. It was late and undercover surveillance wasn't very exciting.

"Here we go," Pete said softly.

A black-clad figure emerged from the shadows and approached the park bench. His head turned as he scanned the surrounding area. Apparently satisfied that he was alone, he took his time with the envelope, pulling a penlight from his pocket to study the document and make sure it was what he wanted. He raised his arm and a bent figure staggered forward, propelled by a shove. Mrs. Entwhistle gasped. It was Giancarlo.

What was wrong with him, though? He didn't seem to have a face and his hands were bound behind him. He was pushed down on the bench with some force; they heard the grunt.

"Lock the doors behind us," Pete whispered to Mrs. Entwhistle as he, Sheriff Trevino and Dex eased out of the car. The overhead light had been turned off, and they took care not to make noise with the doors. Soundlessly, they moved toward the bench, spreading out to cover as much of the area as possible. Mrs. Entwhistle knew the other three deputies were already in place at entrances to the park. She sat on the edge of her seat, watching breathlessly.

"Show me your hands! Show me your hands!"

Mrs. Entwhistle would never have believed Pete could roar like that. She was shocked. Sheriff Trevino and Dex both yelled, too. The man at the park bench jumped up, assessed the odds against him, and obediently raised his arms over his head. The lawmen swarmed him, cuffing him as he lay on his face on the grass.

So engrossed were the men with subduing their captive that nobody noticed another man running toward the parking lot. Nobody but Mrs. Entwhistle. She couldn't let him get away. From her perch on the back seat, she leaned forward and applied the heel of her hand to the horn. The blast ripped the night air, and she saw Dex look up, see the running man and leap to his feet in pursuit. He caught up with him just as the deputy sheriff posted at the parking entrance reached them. There was a tangle of arms and legs, along with a lot of yelling, because this one didn't give up easily. But finally he lay face down and handcuffed, like his companion.

Mrs. Entwhistle thought it was safe to get out of the car then, for Giancarlo plainly needed her. Her legs had pins-and-needles from nervousness and so much sitting, but she walked it off and made her way to the park bench, stepping gingerly around the prisoner.

"Giancarlo, are you okay?" She saw, as she bent over him, that the reason he seemed not to have a face was that a bag had been placed over his head. She pulled it off, revealing, of all things, an enormous grin on his wizened yellow face.

"Sure, I'm okay. Did you see what happened?"

"Yes, your captives sat you on the bench and then..."

"It all went off according to plan," Giancarlo crowed triumphantly

"Whose plan?"

"Why, mine, of course. I had 'em just where I wanted 'em, and now, thanks to me, they've been caught."

~*~

Giancarlo had a lot more to say, but unfortunately it didn't make much sense. He said he'd persuaded his captors to take him along to the park for the drop, instead of being left beside the road somewhere. His story got fuzzy after that; it was hard to see how he'd done anything except get kidnapped by a couple of hoodlums on order of his former business partners. But in his own mind, he was a hero.

Pete listened patiently to the gush of words, then rubbed his chin noncommittally. "Well, Mr. Cicerino, I guess we'd better get you home to your daughter's. She's worried about you."

Mrs. Entwhistle's eyebrows arched. *Take him home to Sissy? Why, he was part of the gang; shouldn't he be taken to jail? Was he just going to get away with it, like his daughter? What kind of justice was that?*

Pete continued. "Sheriff Trevino may have some questions for you, but I think he'll agree they can wait until tomorrow."

Sheriff Trevino nodded, helped Giancarlo to his feet, and, with an arm around his waist, escorted him to a patrol car for a ride home.

"Are you just going to let him go?" Mrs. Entwhistle demanded of Pete.

"He's facing a mightier justice than anything we can provide," Pete said soberly. "I doubt he'd live a week in a jail cell. In fact, I doubt if he'll live much more than a week outside of one."

"You're right, of course you are." Mrs. Entwhistle felt ashamed of herself. She'd gotten so caught up in the right and wrong of Giancarlo's situation, she'd forgotten to be compassionate. "His last days should be spent with his family. He's certainly not a flight risk or a threat to anyone else."

Suddenly, she was as tired as she'd ever been in her life. Her legs actually felt like they might just give out and deposit her on the ground. Dex was at her side in an instant, taking her arm and helping her to her car. He slid behind the wheel and, with Pete following, they drove slowly to Mrs. Entwhistle's house in the silence of exhaustion. With Dex and Pete supporting her on each side, she made her way into the house, where they helped her into Floyd's big old recliner. She noticed her clothes, the ones Dex had worn, slung over the back of the sofa, the hat on the seat where anyone might sit on it, but she didn't care. Just this once, she'd wait to tidy up until morning. Pete tucked a quilt around her shoulders, turned off all but the hall light, and he and Dex tiptoed away. Mrs. Entwhistle didn't stir until sunrise.

Then, with groans and starts and stops, she levered herself out of the chair and into the kitchen. Roger needed to go out and then have his breakfast. All this took a lot longer than it used to. Mrs. Entwhistle stood at the screen door with her coffee cup while Roger made many sniffing trips around the back yard before he found the perfect spot to deposit his pee. Then she heated his soft dog food in the microwave until it was exactly the right temperature. Bending down to place his dish before him elicited another groan. Police work sure took it out of a person.

At last, the old dog was ready to go back to sleep, and Mrs. Entwhistle could head upstairs for a long, hot bath. After a restorative big breakfast, she felt ready to meet the day. She paused for a moment when she realized what lay ahead: a very difficult conversation with Jimmy Jack.

Arriving at the *Pantograph*, she saw Dex's scooter parked by the door. He must have gotten there early to snag that plum parking space. She knew how annoyed the other reporters would be to see the little Vespa taking up a whole space. Inside, Dex was hunched over his computer in palpable concentration. She didn't bother him, just walked on into Jimmy Jack's office. He motioned for her to close the door and take a seat, not rising with his customary courtesy when she entered.

"Talk," he said shortly.

She did.

"So, you see, Giancarlo was working with the syndicate that was trying to place wind turbines on Booger's land so they could launder money, probably drug money. When things didn't go as planned, they hired two thugs to kidnap Giancarlo. They thought if they applied enough muscle, they could get their own way, but they didn't figure on Booger. He got suspicious and changed his mind, getting himself a beating for his trouble. If they'd had any sense, they'd have given up then, but I guess they didn't realize who they were dealing with. If they knew Booger, they'd have known that you can't tell him anything. He was just the same in first grade. Nobody was going to make him stop eating boogers until he was good and ready."

Jimmy Jack's head was in his hands. He didn't raise his eyes as he said, "And Mr. Cicerino?"

"He's dying, Jimmy Jack, I mean Mr. McNamara. The sheriff let him go home to Sissy's. He doesn't have long; there's no point in punishing him."

"What about the people behind Winterberry Wind Farms?"

"Pete says the FBI and the Treasury Department are working on finding out who they are. It's likely the men they hired to do their dirty work will rat out their employers. They committed assault and kidnapping, and that could mean a life sentence, Pete said, so he thinks they'll be ready to exchange information for a plea deal. They're not too smart, but they're that smart."

"And Butch and Sissy?"

"Well." Mrs. Entwhistle paused, eyebrows raised. "I guess they've worked out their difficulties."

"Meaning?"

"The Booster Club funds have been replaced with no one the wiser. Except the person who's been putting all those comments in the Palaver. I wonder if we'll ever know who that was."

"Oh, I know who it was," Jimmy Jack said. "I had the e-mail trail traced back to the sender. It was Butch."

"Butch! He planted those items? What was he trying

to do?"

"I'm not exactly sure," Jimmy Jack said. "Maybe just bring things to a head? Scare Sissy into getting some sense? It worked, didn't it?"

"Well, I swanee," Mrs. Entwhistle said. "I guess it did, at that."

Dex Shoots; He Scores

When Jimmy Jack's phone rang, Mrs.Entwhistle took the opportunity to leave his office and check on Dex. He looked up when she entered the newsroom. His young face was drawn with exhaustion, and there were blue circles under his eyes. She noticed he was wearing the same clothes he'd had on last night.

"Did you work all night?" she asked, sitting down beside him.

"I did. I had to get this story written while it was fresh in my mind," Dex said, rubbing his neck. "I want you to read it. Here, sit in my chair and read it on the screen. If you see anything wrong, holler. I'm going to get some coffee."

Mrs. Entwhistle obediently sat in Dex's chair, trying

to ignore the fact that it was still warm. This was no time to indulge one of her little phobias. She began reading.

Half an hour later, she looked up from the screen at Dex's nervous but hopeful face. "It's brilliant!" she said. She stood and hugged him.

"Is it really okay?" he asked.

"It's better than okay," she said, "it's as good a piece of investigative reporting as I've ever read. Anywhere. I can't wait to see it in print."

"Well, you won't see it in the *Pantograph*," a voice behind them said. Jimmy Jack had spoken.

"Why in the world not?" Mrs. Entwhistle asked.

"I told you both to stick to teas and PTA meetings. I told you to leave the investigative reporting alone, that this is a small-town newspaper, and I'm not about to shake up this town with sensationalism."

Dex looked devastated. "Have you read my article, sir?" he asked in a shaky voice.

"Yeah, I read it just now. It's great writing, Dex, and I congratulate you on that. It's just not what I'm paying you for."

"Actually, sir, you're not paying me at all. I'm a

summer intern."

"All the more reason not to run your piece."

Mrs. Entwhistle wished she had her cane with her. It would have been the perfect time to thump it on the floor. Or thump Jimmy Jack upside his indolent, indecisive, ignorant head. But this was no time to get mad. Tact was needed.

"Mr. McNamara, may I speak to you privately?" she asked in her sweetest, grandmotherly tones.

For a moment, she thought Jimmy Jack was going to refuse, but then he jerked his head toward his office and stalked off in that direction. She followed, taking careful note of his body language. His chin was tucked, he was viewing the world over the top of his glasses, his arms were folded across his chest, and he was taking longer than usual strides. Why, he's scared! Mrs. Entwhistle thought. And defensive. Let's see what that's about.

She settled herself in a chair across the desk from her disgruntled editor and sat up very straight. Both feet were firmly on the floor, and she rested her hands, palms cupped, in her lap. Taking a deep breath, she relaxed her shoulders back and down, away from her ears. She allowed a beat or two to pass while she sat peacefully, and was gratified to see Jimmy Jack uncross his arms. He was relaxing a bit, too.

"Now, honey, tell me what's bothering you," Mrs. Entwhistle said, smiling at him the way she did when he was a six-year-old with missing front teeth, when he was just the cutest thing since crickets. She'd known Jimmy Jack all his life and he *had* been a cute, if timid, kid. The same timid behavior wasn't so cute in an adult, but she focused on the little boy who still lived behind the grown-up façade.

"Look, Mrs. Entwhistle, I appreciate all the work you've done, and how you've taken Dex under your wing. Although that was probably not a good thing, considering the mess you've gotten yourselves into."

"Tell me where we went wrong," Mrs. Entwhistle said humbly.

"Well... Well, you were supposed to cover community activities."

"Which we did."

"And not get into all that other stuff."

"When I started out, I was just checking into the Booster Club discrepancies that I picked up on at a school board meeting. Then I interviewed Booger about the wind turbine farm for a story that I believe you assigned me." She paused to give Jimmy Jack a chance to say something. He remained silent, staring down at his blotter.

"So one thing just led to another. The wind farm had something to do with the Booster Club, which had something to do with Sissy and Butch and Giancarlo."

"You went to Booger's house in the middle of the night and broke in," Jimmy Jack said, holding his head in both hands.

"Now, we did not break in," Mrs. Entwhistle said firmly, "I told Dex I wouldn't break in, and we did not. Besides, Caleb gave us permission to look around."

"Did he give you permission to wiggle through the dog door?" Jimmy Jack asked, daring to be just a touch sarcastic.

Mrs. Entwhistle had had quite enough. "I take responsibility for my actions, not that there is anyone else objecting to them besides you. Booger and his boys are grateful for our help; Pete Peters, Deputy U.S. Marshall, is grateful for our help; Sheriff Trevino is grateful for our help; and Butch, Sissy and Giancarlo are grateful for our help. What is your problem?"

Jimmy Jack raised his head and tried, but failed, to meet her eye. "Look, I just want to run a little small-town paper. No big stories, no controversies, no ulcers, no lawsuits, no Molotov cocktails thrown through my window. We don't know who's behind all this, but they ain't good guys, that's for sure."

Mrs. Entwhistle smiled. "When Diane was four, she took ballet lessons, and I remember her teacher passing out dolls as props for one of the dances. The girls all had definite ideas about which doll they wanted, but she told them, 'You get what you get, and you don't have a fit.' I always remembered that. It applies to so much in life, don't you think? This messy story, this is what you got. Now you have to find a way to deal with it."

Jimmy Jack's hunted eyes would have touched a far harder heart than Mrs. Entwhistle's. She recognized that he needed time to think.

"Dex and I are going over to the Busy Bee and have a big, gooey donut," she said. "Can we bring you back anything? No? Well, then we'll see you in about half an hour."

She collected Dex, shushing his protestations that they needed to confront Jimmy Jack, needed to insist, demand, plead, beg. As they left the newsroom, she glanced back at Jimmy Jack's office.

Through the big window she saw him put his head down on his desk. Just like a first-grader at rest-time, she thought, and felt a pang of sympathy for him. It's hard to grow up, she reflected, whether you're six or thirty-six.

Mrs. Entwhistle brought Jimmy Jack back a donut, anyhow. She thought it would be a good sign if he wanted it after all. He was still at his desk and was thumbing through a yellowed scrapbook of clippings. He looked up when she entered and placed the greasy napkin before him.

"Oh, thanks," he said, immediately unwrapping the donut and taking a big bite. "I was just looking at Dad's old scrapbook. He was pre-computer, you know, kept clippings and pasted them in a book. That's how old-school my dad was."

"Mac was one of my favorite people," Mrs. Entwhistle said.

"I've been thinking what Dad would do if he was still sitting at this desk."

"Yes? And?"

"Dad would go for it. He'd run Dex's article at the top of the front page with a black banner headline above it, and let the chips fall where they may."

"Hmm." Mrs. Entwhistle was noncommittal. She knew when to stand back.

"Only he'd say, 'let the shit hit the fan,'" Jimmy Jack said with a grin. "Oh, excuse me, Mrs. Entwhistle."

"I've heard the expression before."

Jimmy Jack stood and stretched mightily. He worked his jaw from side to side, rolled his shoulders up and down, cracked his knuckles and flexed his knees. "I'm gonna do it," he said. "I don't know what will happen, but I'm gonna run Dex's article."

"Good for you!" Mrs. Entwhistle said. "I'm proud of you, honey, and your dad would be, too. And maybe you'll be pleasantly surprised at the results when Dex's piece hits print. You never know."

"Let's let 'er rip."

You Just Never Know

Dex took Mrs. Entwhistle's front steps two at a time and hammered on her door so hard even Roger heard. She hurried to answer, with Roger barking at her feet.

"Why, Dex, what in the world?"

"Mrs. E., look here, you'll never guess what, just look at this!" Dex said in one breath, shaking a sheet of paper under her nose.

"Well, hold still, then, let me see. Why, Dex!" She had to sit down. "Why, Dex, it's a letter from the *Washington Post*. And... let's see... They say congratulations on your outstanding journalism... Ground-breaking reporting... Remarkable for a young reporter -- and they're offering you a job! Just as soon as you graduate, you can go to work for the *Washington Post!*" Mrs. Entwhistle fanned herself with the letter. She felt all over prickly cold and hot.

Dex rescued his letter and smoothed it carefully. "I can't believe it. To get a job offer like this one before I even graduate. It's unbelievable."

"I believe it," Mrs. Entwhistle said. "If ever a boy deserved it, you do. I'm so happy for you." She heard her voice go thin with emotion and felt tears prickle behind her eyes.

"I just had to let you know first thing," Dex said, "before I even called my folks. We did it together, Mrs. E. I couldn't have done it without you helping me along."

"Aw, shoot, you couldn't be stopped," Mrs. Entwhistle laughed. "I just stood back and let you go. This job offer will change your life, you know. Why, you'll be up in the big city with all those high-powered movers and shakers. Floyd used to call them the lizard loafer crowd. Do you reckon you'll become one of them? Get you some fancy shoes and forget your small-town friends?"

"I don't know about the fancy shoes, but I can guarantee I won't forget my small-town friends," Dex said, shaking his head and laughing with her. "No matter how hard I try! Are you going to continue to ridicule me, or are you ready to go to the party?"

"I guess we might ought to check out that party."

Jimmy Jack was throwing one for his staff and had invited the entire community. He'd commandeered the same park where the kidnappers had been apprehended.

"I'll meet you there, though, because I'll have to walk

over," Mrs. Entwhistle said, "My car's on the fritz; it wouldn't start this morning. I don't know what's the matter, but I'll have one of the guys at the garage take a look at it tomorrow."

"No walking for you," Dex said, "you'll ride with me."

"Did you get a car?"

"No, ma'am, but this will be more fun than a car."

Dex led her to the curb where his scooter was leaning on its stand.

"Oh, honey, I don't think so," Mrs. Entwhistle protested.

"Do you think you're too old?" Dex asked with a challenging grin.

The words were hardly out of his mouth when Mrs. Entwhistle hiked her leg over the seat, thankful that she had on her third-best pantsuit. Dex plunked his helmet on her head, rendering her blind and speechless for a moment until she adjusted it. He jumped on the kick-start and the little scooter came to life. It was small, it didn't go very fast, but it was the first time Mrs. Entwhistle had ridden on a scooter and she found it exhilarating. She hung on tight and whooped as they puttered along the quiet streets.

The sun was still hot, but the trees in the park were beginning to show the first sprays of autumn color among their green boughs. Beneath them were long tables covered in red and white checked cloths, groaning under a spread of food. The air was perfumed with the smoke of several barbeque grills tended by sweating men in white aprons who served up ribs, hamburgers and hot dogs. Friends and neighbors congregated beside coolers brimming with iced bottles, where Jimmy Jack was passing out drinks and urging people to fill their plates. He paused in his hostly duties when Dex pulled the scooter up with a flourish and helped Mrs. Entwhistle dismount. A cheer went up, much to her discomfort.

Jimmy Jack put an arm around each of them and walked them to a portable stage where a bluegrass band was assembling. He held them there and addressed the crowd.

"Friends, here are the stars of the show, Dex Shofield and Cora Entwhistle."

Jimmy Jack had got himself a portable microphone of some kind, and his amplified voice echoed eerily throughout the park. There was a deafening screech of feedback, and he adjusted the mike in his lapel.

"I'm proud to announce today that the *Pantograph* has been awarded the Ralph J. Teeter Award for Excellence in Local Reporting."

Dex and Mrs. Entwhistle exchanged glances of amazement. This was news to them, although since Dex's story ran, they'd received media attention from national outlets. They'd been interviewed by big city reporters, and sat together in front of Leslie Stahl when she'd come to town for "Sixty Minutes." That interview never did air, but they agreed it was a lot of fun, and Leslie was just as nice as can be. Far from becoming blasé at all the attention, they'd grown increasingly incredulous.

"I'm just a college kid," Dex would say wonderingly.

"And I'm just an old lady," Mrs. Entwhistle would echo. "Who'd 'a thought it?"

Dex's job offer and now this award! Mrs. Entwhistle was overwhelmed. Jimmy Jack continued.

"A small-town newspaper typically covers local events, school activities and sports teams. When I hired Mrs. Entwhistle, I was perfectly content to go on doing that. But she had other ideas, and we all know her to be an unstoppable force. With the addition of Dex Shofield, you might say my fate was sealed. Together, they sniffed out one of the biggest stories ever to hit our town. And I'll admit, I fought them all the way. I lacked the vision my father had, and the courage. But Mrs. Entwhistle wasn't having any of my excuses. She gave me the kick in the pants I needed, and for that I'll always be grateful.

"Newspapers are often overlooked now that we get so much of our information from television and the Internet. But we should always remember that a free press is a powerful hammer in democracy's tool kit. A newspaper's mandate is to speak truth to power, and to do it regardless of the consequences. Reporters are committed to bringing you unbiased, honest information, whether they work for the *New York Times* or the *Pantograph*. We do it because we love it. To receive an award for doing what we love is just icing on the cake. The real reward is having the trust of our readers, our friends, and neighbors.

Thank you for coming to help us celebrate. I'm honored that you're here.

"While we're celebrating today – and this is so often how life works, isn't it? – we're saddened to learn one of our own, one who grew up here but lived most of his life in California, has passed away. Giancarlo Cicerino died last night at the home of his daughter and son-in-law, Sissy and Butch Smith. Sissy and Butch will be letting us know about funeral arrangements, and in the meantime, I'm sure they'd appreciate your support."

There were narrowed eyes and pursed lips among the onlookers. They knew that Giancarlo had been mixed up with some unsavory people whose plans did not include the town's welfare. His self-congratulatory story of masterminding the apprehension of his kidnappers leaked like an old rowboat. The town was divided on whether someone as sick as Giancarlo should be punished or allowed to skate. Some heated discussions raised the temperature in the Busy Bee Diner. Now death had settled that question.

Sissy and Butch wore a whiff of suspicion that would haunt them to their graves. But nothing had been proven, no charges had been filed, so their neighbors would give them the benefit of the doubt. They'd carry casseroles to Sissy and buy drinks for Butch, and if there was a local memorial service for Giancarlo, they'd turn out. That was just the way small towns operated when there was a death in the family. But maybe, they agreed quietly among themselves, they'd vote for somebody else to be the next president of the Booster Club. And maybe they'd check out the new insurance agency that just opened in the next town. After all, actions have consequences.

"Now I'd like to invite you all to come and get a plate of this excellent food," Jimmy Jack continued. "The Busy Bee Diner catered this spread for us, so you're sure to find your favorite dishes. Again, thank you for coming."

Jimmy Jack unclipped the mike and mopped his face with a large, white handkerchief. "Whew! That's thirsty work," he said, popping the cap off a bottle of beer and heading for a shade tree.

Mrs. Entwhistle and Dex accepted congratulations from their friends and neighbors, telling over and over again how they ran down their story. Dex showed off his *Washington Post* letter and promised to keep in touch after he became a big-time reporter. Mrs. Entwhistle insisted that Dex get all the credit.

"I just helped a bit," she said. "Dex wrote the story."

She saw Maxine waving from the covered pavilion, went to join her and dropped into a folding chair grateful to be out of the sun. "Well, Max, what do you think of all this?"

Before Maxine could answer, a deeper voice spoke. "Cora, ain't you just the one!"

It was Booger, scrubbed, slicked, combed and emitting waves of aftershave. He wore new overalls so stiff they looked like they could have walked there without him. Caleb and Nate stood at their father's side, and all three beamed down at Mrs. Entwhistle. Booger jerked his chin and Caleb obediently placed a chair on Mrs. Entwhistle's other side. Booger settled himself with a creaking of denim, looking like a man who was prepared to stay all day. His sons drifted off in the direction of the food.

"It's a durn good thing I didn't get no wind turbines on my farm," Booger said. "'Cause now Caleb thinks he might do a mite bit of farming. He ain't got no job, and being home for a while, he kinda remembered what he liked about farming. Bein' his own boss, out in the open all day, don't have to answer to nobody – well, 'cept'n his Daddy. I'm just as tickled as a little pink pig in the sunshine to have him back home."

"Yes, it solves a lot of problems, doesn't it?" Mrs. Entwhistle said. "You can stay in your house and have somebody there to look after you."

"Not that I *need* it," Booger said. "I was doin' just fine on my own."

He seemed to have forgotten his recent hospitalizations and the ride to the emergency room in Mrs. Entwhistle's car. She remembered; she still hadn't completely gotten the odor out of the upholstery. On humid days, she was reminded of Booger.

"Now, thing is, sometimes a man can get lonely, even if'n he has his kin all around him." Booger looked off into the horizon, his big face the picture of innocence. "Like, myself, fer instance. I always enjoyed the company of a purty woman." He gave Mrs. Entwhistle a meaningful look.

Her eyes widened in horrified realization at where the conversation was headed. Maxine suddenly developed a coughing fit that made her eyes water so much she had to wipe them with a tissue. Mrs. Entwhistle shot her a disgusted look. She was no help at all.

"Well, yes, we all, uh, like to have, er, friends," Mrs. Entwhistle stammered.

"And if'n there was a lady, say maybe a wider-lady, that'd like to set a spell on the porch of an evening, maybe have a dish of ice cream or a little sip of 'shine, why, that'd sure be nice."

"Mm, uh huh. Excuse me, Booger, Maxine, I need to, uh, just check on something. Over there. I might be a while."

Mrs. Entwhistle beat a hasty retreat across the sun-parched park grass to where Dex was standing with a group of men. "Pssst, Dex! C'mere."

"Yeah, sure, what is it, Mrs. E.?"

"I think Booger has designs on me," she whispered. "He's – what do you call it? – hitting on me."

"Why, Mrs. E., what could be more fitting? He's got a lot to offer, including a fruit cellar full of vintage peaches, and a doggie-door just built for you."

"Dexter Schofield, you stop it! I came to you for sympathy, not ridicule."

"Then it's your lucky day, because you get both!" Dex said, laughing in her face.

She couldn't help but laugh with him. What would she do without him when he went back to school? She decided not to think about it. Today was a day for celebrating. Besides, she had something else on her mind.

"There is one other thing, though," she said. "I'm thinking about buying something and I'd like to get your opinion."

"Sure. What is it?"

"Well, my car is old and cranky, and I purely hate to spend money on a new one at my age. So I was thinking a scooter might be just the thing for short hops around town. But do you think I'm too old to ride one?"

"Mrs. E., I think you could ride the wind."

The End.

About the Author

Doris Reidy began her writing career in third grade, when a poem about fairies dancing in the moonlight made the local newspaper. (Rumor suggests it was a slow news day). In later years, she wrote non-fiction articles for *Redbook*, *Writer's Digest* and *Atlanta Magazine*, among others, and a monthly book review column for the *Atlanta Journal and Constitution*. Then came a long silence during which life intervened, followed by a second act as a novelist. After writing three novels, **Five for the Money** (nominated for the 2016 Georgia Author of the Year/First Novel award), **Every Last Stitch** (nominated for the 2017 Georgia Author of the Year Award, Literary Fiction), and Imperfect Stranger (nominated for the 2018 Georgia Author of the Year Award, Literary Fiction), she found a friend and muse in *Mrs. Entwhistle*. Please follow Doris Reidy on Facebook, her website, www.dorisreidy.com, and leave your feedback at reidybooks@gmail.com.

Turn the page for a bonus feature: The first of the short stories in the original **Mrs. Entwhistle** collection, wherein the world meets this remarkable lady, and can't help but wonder when she will decides to take control....

Mrs. Entwhistle Buys A Car

One of the worst days of her life was when her son took her car away. She didn't say that lightly, for Mrs. Entwhistle had had some bad days in her seventy-eight years. There was the day of Floyd's heart attack. The day she'd witnessed that horrible wreck on the interstate. The time Tommy got hit by a car, and she was so scared she couldn't get her breath, but it turned out his only injury was a broken arm. Awful days, every one of them, but this ranked right up there with them.

Driving meant freedom. She could get in her big Buick and go to the drugstore to get her pills whenever she needed to. She could get her hair done and visit her best friend and go to the library. Lord knows, she wasn't planning to drive to Florida, she reflected bitterly. So why did Tommy have to get so bossy and officious and tell her she wasn't safe on the road anymore, and to hand over her keys. Now.

Please. And Diane just sat there nodding.

They'd both appeared unexpectedly at her door on a Saturday afternoon, looking sheepish but determined. Choosing to sit in the front room instead of the kitchen to give their visit extra weight, she supposed, they settled in for the kill.

Just because she'd had a couple—well, three—little fender-benders in the last year or two. Okay, in the last six months. Still, those accidents could have happened to a person of any age. That stop sign, for instance, was all covered over with kudzu. How was she supposed to guess it was there? When she backed into another car at Kroger's, it was just a kiss between bumpers; you could hardly see the dent. That rude, screechy woman had gone on and on about thousands of dollars for a brand-new car and now look! People shouldn't pay so much for cars anyway. A Ford or Chevy was good enough for anybody. She only drove the Buick because that's what Floyd left her when he died.

The last accident, she was prepared to admit, was more serious. She'd been looking down to get a tissue from her purse and wham, she smacked right into the car ahead of her. Got a big goose egg on her forehead that turned into a black eye. The other driver was polite enough, but he kept repeating over and over in a most tiresome manner that he was just sitting there at a traffic light, minding his own business, and pow! She'd declined an ambulance and accepted a ticket, which she paid and hoped nobody would find out. But, of course, her nosy children knew all about it. Mrs. Entwhistle felt cross with them. More than cross: disappointed and maybe a little bit heart-broken.

She wasn't one to go down without a fight. She told Tommy and Diane that teenage drivers with their crazy speeding caused more serious accidents than senior citizens; she'd read that somewhere. She pointed out that nobody forbade them to drive. Diane countered that teenager drivers keep getting better, whereas older folks...Her mother's glare could still stop Diane in her tracks.

Mrs. Entwhistle bargained, promising to only drive close to home.

"All your accidents happened within a mile or two of home," Tommy said.

She blustered. "Who do you think you are, telling me what I can and can't do? I am still your mother." They were unmoved.

She reminded them of the inconvenience to themselves: "You'll have to get time off work for my doctor appointments and take me grocery shopping on your precious Saturdays."

"We'll work it out. We'll have a schedule," Diane replied.

To her shame, she pleaded. "Please, don't make me a prisoner in my own house."

Diane wavered then, but that Tommy, he was hard as a rock. "No, Mother, we won't let you hurt yourself or someone else. It's time to stop driving."

He drove her Buick away, and that was that.

But he'd neglected to deprive her of her perfectly valid driver's license. Certainly, she didn't wish to hurt anyone and she didn't intend to. But what she did intend to do was keep driving. She had money in savings. Mrs. Entwhistle would simply buy herself a car.

The first thing to figure out was how to get to a car dealership now that she couldn't drive there. A resident of suburbia all her life, Mrs. Entwhistle had never ridden on a city bus. Not that there were any bus lines in her neighborhood. Taxis were expensive and you didn't know exactly how much they cost until the driver told you, because who could read all that fine print on the door? Maybe she'd ask her best friend, Maxine, to take her. Her children hadn't lifted her driving privileges. Yet. Mrs. Entwhistle dialed the phone.

"Hello?"

"Max, it's Cora. Are you busy?"

"No, not a bit, just sitting here watching the birds at my feeder."

"Any good ones?"

"I think I saw a red-tail hawk. It wasn't at the feeder, but I heard a whole lot of squawking and way up in the tree, I saw an awfully big bird. Couldn't see it real well, but I bet that's what it was."

"Yes, probably. Listen, Max, I was wondering if I

could ask a big favor."

"Sure, honey, what is it?"

"I need a ride to the Ford dealer out on the four-lane."

"Did your car break down?"

"No, not exactly. What it is, Tommy and Diane decided I can't drive any more. They took my car away."

"No! They did not!"

"But they did. And gave me a big lecture on how I'm a danger to myself and others. That's what they said: a danger to myself and others. I never would have believed that I raised children who could be so disrespectful and ugly-acting."

"Now, Cora, don't get in a fuss. Children think they know it all and we know nothing, no matter what age they are. Why, your driving's just fine. You've had a couple of little boo-boos but no real harm done."

"So, will you take me to the car place? I'm going to get me a new car."

"Why, sure, I will. Won't that be fun! A new car."

~*~

When Maxine tapped her car horn in the driveway at ten the next morning, Mrs. Entwhistle emerged from her house promptly. She wore what she thought of as her marryin' and buryin' suit, which she'd livened up for today's important transaction with a bright pink scarf. She felt nervous. Floyd had always handled big things like car-buying. In fact, he was such a ferocious bargainer that Mrs. Entwhistle refused to accompany him on car-buying missions. It was too embarrassing. The resulting purchases were often not to her liking, but it was a man's place to buy cars and he knew best. Now she was stepping into an unfamiliar arena, but only because she had to. Thanks to her kids.

"Cora, look there. The carnival's in town," Maxine said as they neared the fairground. "Let's go in just for a minute and see if that fortune teller from last year is still there. She told me some really good stuff."

"What?"

"I don't exactly remember, but it was good. Do you mind if we run in and see?"

"You're the driver," Mrs. Entwhistle said agreeably, although she was thinking she'd never done such a thing as visit a fortune teller in her life. But Maxine was a free spirit and that was one of things she liked about her.

There weren't many cars in the parking lot at that early hour, enabling Maxine to maneuver her enormous Lincoln Navigator into a conveniently wide spot. She'd picked out that car herself, one of the first things she did after her husband died. It might just be a tad too big for Max to handle easily, since she sat so low in the driver's seat she could *hardly see over the steering wheel. But it was her choice, and let it be an example for me,* Mrs.

Entwhistle thought, as she struggled down from the high seat. *If Max can do it, I can do it.*

The ladies set out on the midway, resolutely ignoring the bewitching aroma of funnel cakes. They had walked the entire length and Mrs. Entwhistle's feet were protesting – she was wearing her good shoes, after all – when they finally came to a tent set off by itself.

"Madame Esmeralda the Magnificent," read the banner over the door. No one was stirring and the place looked deserted, but Maxine was not easily deterred.

"Yoo-hoo!" she called, poking her head inside the tent. "Madame Esmeralda, are you there? Are you open?"

Draperies at the back of the tent stirred and a tousled woman wearing a bedraggled housecoat appeared. "I'm open now," she said, around a huge yawn. "You ladies here for a reading?"

"You're not Madame Esmeralda. I saw her last year, and you're not her," Max said, her disappointment making her more blunt than usual.

"Madame Esmeraldas come and go," the woman said. "I'm Madame Esmeralda this year. Do you or don't you want your fortunes told?"

"Well. I don't know, now. I thought you'd be the real Madame Esmeralda. What do you think, Cora?"

"We walked all this way. You might as well."

"Are you not going to?"

"Oh, I don't think so. I really don't believe in that stuff. No offense," Mrs. Entwhistle added, with an apologetic glance at Madame Esmeralda.

"None taken," Madame said. She motioned to Maxine. "Please come and sit down at the table and let me consult the spirits. And that will be five dollars."

Maxine rummaged through all the pockets in her pocket book, finally extracting the requisite bill, and then settled herself in the small chair at the table. Madame Esmeralda bent low over the cloudy globe.

"The spirits are stirring," she intoned. "I see the figure of a small animal - is it a dog?"

"Yes! That's Jingo, he died last spring."

"Jingo wants me to tell you that he is happy in his heavenly home and is waiting for you."

"Awww. Bless his heart, I miss him."

Madame Esmeralda gazed some more, biting back another yawn. "You will get a new dog," she finally said, "and it will be an even better dog than Jingo. He says that's okay."

Max nodded eagerly. Mrs. Entwhistle knew she'd been thinking about getting a puppy, or maybe an older rescue dog.

"And I see a...wait, who's getting a new car?"

"Why, I am," Mrs. Entwhistle said. "We're on our way to the car place right now."

"Hmmmm. Not a good idea," Madame Esmeralda

said flatly. "I see great danger and it has something to do with a new car. The spirits are not always plain."

"You sound just like my children," Mrs. Entwhistle said. "I can drive as well as anyone. Mind your own business and tell the spirits to mind theirs. No offense."

"Again, none taken," Madam said, "but I'm not kidding, I really did see something about an accident or something bad, and it involved a car."

"Well, thank you very much. I guess you want five dollars from me, now," Mrs. Entwhistle said in an icy voice.

"Nope, that one's on the house," Madame replied.

After more predictions about sudden wealth and the possibility of a remarriage for Maxine, the ladies took their leave of Madame Esmeralda and hiked the long way back to the car.

"I might get another dog, but I don't think I'll remarry, though," Maxine said thoughtfully. "Once was plenty, you know?"

~*~

The Ford sedans were lined up in rows in front of the dealership. They sparkled in the sunlight like multi-colored gems. Maxine parked the Lincoln and she and Mrs. Entwhistle approached the front door. Inside, a huddle of men in suits and ties were laughing uproariously. As if that wasn't intimidating enough, all the men looked around at their entrance and fell silent, as if someone had flipped the "off" switch. Feeling like interlopers who'd just spoiled a good time, the ladies paused uncertainly.

A very young man detached himself from the huddle and approached them.

"Good morning, ladies, may I help you?"

"Yes, I'd like to look at cars," Mrs. Entwhistle said.

"I see. Will your husband be joining you?"

"I hope not. He's been in the grave for seven years now."

"Oh, sorry, I just thought...I meant...usually...never mind. What can I show you today?"

"I want to see your cheapest Ford sedan with an automatic transmission." Mrs. Entwhistle could drive a stick-shift, Floyd had taught her, but she'd be darned if she would, now that the choice was up to her. "And I want green," she added.

"I think we have just the thing," the young man said. "I'm John Mackey, by the way."

"The same Mackey that's on the sign?"

"That's my Dad. I'm Junior, but he's taught me a lot about cars and I'm sure I can help you."

John ushered them out into the car lot and led them to a forest green, four-door sedan. It had fancy chrome wheels – "mag wheels," John said - which Mrs. Entwhistle knew would be a bugger to keep clean, but the green paint shone with a beautiful intensity that won her heart.

"That's the one, I want that one," she said.

"Well, don't you want to drive it first?" John asked.

"Oh, yes, of course, I should drive it," Mrs. Entwhistle said, looking at Maxine doubtfully.

"Go on, now, Cora, let's just take a little spin and see how it feels to you."

"Uh, do you - you do have a driver's license?" John asked.

"I certainly do, young man," Mrs. Entwhistle replied, giving him the glare she'd so often directed successfully at her own children. It worked on him, too.

With no further chat about licenses, they piled into the car, Mrs. Entwhistle behind the wheel, John beside her in the front seat, and Maxine in the back. After adjusting the mirrors and pulling up the seat so that John's knees were jack-knifed against the dashboard, Mrs. Entwhistle turned the key in the ignition and slowly, slowly, backed out of the parking space. She crept through the car lot and paused for long moments at the entrance to the highway, looking left, then right, then left, then right. Finally, with no cars in sight in either direction, she pulled out at a dignified pace.

"She'll go a little faster," John said.

Mrs. Entwhistle pressed on the gas and the green car leapt forward, snapping their heads back. "Oops, sorry," she said, "it's got more juice than my old car had."

Now that she'd speeded up, the car felt great. The tires hummed over the roadway, the large windshield gave her a panoramic view and the new seat hit her back in just the right place. Her confidence grew.

"Oh, I like this car!" she said. "I'm going to buy it, for sure. How much is it?"

John quoted a price and glanced apologetically at Mrs. Entwhistle. But she was unfazed.

"I'll take it," she said.

"Really? Don't you want to, maybe, bargain a little bit? Talk about trade-in and all that? That's kind of how it works."

"No, I don't believe in that bargaining stuff. If that's the price, then that's the price. I'm sure you wouldn't cheat me." She peered over at John. "I have the money, you know."

"The road! Watch the road! Okay, that's better. Sorry I yelled. I'd love to sell you this car, but...are you sure?"

"Yes, young man, I'm sure."

"Okay, then. I guess we should head back to the dealership."

"Where can I make a right turn? I don't make left turns."

"Do you make U-turns?"

"Certainly not."

They drove on. None of the right turns looked

suitable to Mrs. Entwhistle. She felt she'd know a safe-looking right turn when she saw one, and she hadn't seen one yet. She swerved to the right at every street to check it out, and then swerved back into her lane.

"Cora." Maxine's voice sounded strange. "Cora, I need to stop. I'm feeling kind of...oh, no!"

Mrs. Entwhistle hit the brakes and came to a lurching stop as the unmistakable odor of vomit filled the car. Maxine opened her door into traffic and the air was torn by the angry blast of a horn. She stumbled out onto the pavement and bent double, retching. John seemed to be paralyzed. Mrs. Entwhistle climbed out from behind the wheel, also into traffic, provoking another horn blast, and helped Maxine over to the side of the road.

"Now, just sit right down on the ground, Max. Here, wipe your chin a little bit. Why, I didn't know you were feeling sick."

"It was the swerving, and being in the back seat," Maxine said huskily, "I just suddenly came over hot and cold and then...I'm so sorry about messing up the car."

"Don't you worry one bit about that. I'm sure John will clean it up."

John was out of the car, too, mopping at his forehead with a white handkerchief and looking like he might throw up himself. He didn't appear to be capable of cleaning much of anything.

"Take your handkerchief and get up as much of that

vomit as you can," Mrs. Entwhistle instructed him. At his appalled look, she said, "Then just throw that hankie away. Do you want to ride with that smell?"

They rolled down all the windows and Mrs. Entwhistle directed John to sit in the back so Maxine could have the front seat. His suggestion that he drive was met with a determined shake of the head. "I'm perfectly capable," Mrs. Entwhistle said. "I just need to find a good right turn."

~*~

"Max, would a Co-Cola help you feel better?"

"I believe it would, Cora, it sounds good."

By now they were far out of town on a sparsely populated stretch of highway. They passed plenty of side roads, but none that Mrs. Entwhistle thought looked promising. There were no restaurants or drive-ins on the right, the only side Mrs. Entwhistle would consider. In vain did John suggest from the back seat that maybe it was time for them to head back. Mrs. Entwhistle ignored him and drove steadily onward. Finally, she spotted a Sonic drive-in off to the right, and immediately braked for a sharp right turn, incurring the wrath of the driver behind her. She drove the short distance to the restaurant, pulled into a space and reached out for the speaker.

"Oops! That should have been fastened better."

John blanched at the sound of metal scraping green paint as Mrs. Entwhistle dropped the speaker down the side of the car. She reeled it in by the cord, bumping all the way up, and pressed the button.

"One Co-Cola, and I believe I'll have a chocolate milkshake. Driving sure makes a person feel empty and I don't remember that we had lunch. John, did you want something?"

"No, ma'am, no thank you. I don't feel so good myself. The smell back here..."

"Okay, then." Into the speaker, she said, "Just bring us the milkshake and Co-Cola."

"Mrs. Entwhistle, now that you've finally made that right turn, it's really time we went back," John said. "I was supposed to meet my...my friend for lunch. She didn't answer when I called to tell her I couldn't make it. She's not good about checking her messages. I expect she'll think I stood her up. She'll be pretty mad."

"Why, of course, John. Just let us drink these and we'll go right back. You should have said you had a date. Is it serious?"

"Maybe, on my part. I don't think it is on hers. She's got lots of men after her, she can have her pick."

"Well, she couldn't do better than you. Don't you think so, Max?"

"Absolutely. He's a good-looking young man. You are, John. And well-spoken, too."

"Yes, and a hard worker with good prospects. Prospects can't get any better than your daddy owning the company," Mrs. Entwhistle said. The ladies laughed companionably. "I guess you'll always drive a good car, too."

"Yes, Dad likes me to drive the latest models; he thinks it's good advertising."

"So there you are: good-looking, well-spoken, hard-working, good prospects and a nice car. You don't have to take a back seat to anybody alive, John Mackey. You're a regular dreamboat. That girl is lucky you'd have her."

Mrs. Entwhistle put the car in reverse, forgetting to wait for removal of the tray on which their drinks had been served. It fell with a clang when the tire rode up over the curb as she backed out.

As she approached the highway, Mrs. Entwhistle came to a full stop. She looked at oncoming traffic long and hard, letting several slow-moving cars pass, and then suddenly shot across the highway onto the southbound lane. Screeching tires and the blasting air-horn of an enormous truck made them all jump.

"Swanee!" she said. "Where did he come from?"

"Cora, maybe we ought to hurry just a little. We have to get home before it gets dark; you know I can't see to drive at night," Maxine said.

Mrs. Entwhistle dutifully pressed down on the gas, gripping the wheel with white knuckles as the speedometer climbed to thirty, forty, fifty, sixty. John shut his eyes and prayed aloud softly: "I've tried to live a good life, Lord, please don't let me die today."

"Truck! Look out!" Maxine screamed. Looming large before them, the signs on the rear of a dump truck hauling gravel warned Stay Back 50 Feet and Not Responsible for Flying Objects. As if on cue, a largish rock flew from the load and smashed into their windshield. Mrs. Entwhistle hit the brakes hard and then fought to control the car's skid. They careened across the road, made a brief foray into the median, then slid all the way back into their original lane. Miraculously, nobody hit them in the course of this wild ride. The car came to rest at last on the edge of a steep embankment. In the sudden quiet, they watched as a hubcap cartwheeled down the hill, chrome glinting in the sun. They listened as the tire slowly deflated—ssssssss—and they felt the car settle with a bump over the flat.

Mrs. Entwhistle broke the silence. "Do you know how to change a tire, John?

~*~

This time she relented when John offered to drive the rest of the way back.

"I am about frazzled," she admitted. "I forgot how nerve-wracking it is to drive. I believe I'll just sit in the back seat, maybe close my eyes for a few minutes."

The sound of her snores soon filled the car. Maxine, too, put her head back and dozed. John squinted through the cracked windshield and drove gingerly on the spare tire. The ladies woke when he rolled gently to a stop at the dealership. Patting back their yawns, they disembarked, straightened their skirts, smoothed their hair and took a firm grip on their purses.

"John, did you fall? What are you doing down there? Are you kissing the ground?"

"No, ma'am, just tying my shoe."

"Well, I've been turning it over in my mind," Mrs. Entwhistle said, "and you know, I don't think I want to buy this car after all. I'd forgotten how exhausting driving can be. I usually just run errands in my neighborhood and my old Buick is fine for that. I believe I'll look into taking a remedial driving course. I know I can pass, and then Tommy will have to give my car back. I don't believe I should drive far, though."

"Why, honey, I'd be happy to take you anyplace you need to go," Maxine said. "I'll probably need to go myself. We'll make a day of it, have lunch and all. It'll be fun. I don't know why we didn't think of it before."

"And I'll buy our lunches," Mrs. Entwhistle said. She wanted to make sure Maxine knew she wasn't just sponging. She could pay her way.

"Well, that's settled then," she continued. "John, thank you kindly for the test ride."

Mrs. Entwhistle hated to see John looking so sad as he surveyed what was left of the new green Ford sedan. There was a long scratch on the driver's door, and the windshield was a web of cracks radiating from a central hole. The even smile of three fat chrome wheels was broken by the skinny black spare, and the back seat reeked of vomit. But really, she thought, a good clean-up with a little buffing would fix almost everything. Surely they were prepared for that at a dealership; it must happen all the time.

"I don't want you to get in trouble about the car getting a few dings and us being gone so long, and then not making a sale," she said. "'Cause you've been real nice."

"No, ma'am," he said. "Don't worry; I'll explain everything to Dad. Everything." He shivered a little.

"Tell your dad I said you're a credit to your raising. And you remember, John, you're a catch. You're a dream-boat."

"Yes, ma'am."

"Come on then, Max. Let's go home before it gets dark."

Made in the USA
Monee, IL
06 November 2020